UNSETTLED

Book One

The Chosen Series

BY ALISA MULLEN

DEDICATIONS

For Mailliw, Shea-Shea, and Bubby

I love you from that part of the sky to that part of the sky to that part of the sky.

Jeanne and Kathy

For your lifelong support to write

A gigantic thank you to Vanessa, Kate and Monika

Kris at Final-Edits.com

I couldn't have done it without you

One

2000

In early May, Boston nightlife was a mixture of rowdy college students savoring a nightly break from their upcoming finals and noises from the Green Line packed full of Red Sox fans who poured out of Fenway Park. The scraping of train rails made the honking cars unnoticeable. Fragrant smells from flowerbeds growing in tiny window boxes of the apartments along Commonwealth Avenue hardly negated the exhaust from the cars and trains.

I held out my hand from the window of Darcy's new black Mercedes Benz. The hot waves of early summer gave Beantown a new surge of vibrancy. I took in a long inhale of the mixture of flowers, exhaust, and the lingering trash cans left out on the sidewalks. I felt my own surge of energy in anticipation for the summer to come.

My name is Lizzie O'Malley and I'd just returned home to start a fresh new life. Later that night, I'd find out that this night out would be the start of a life I'd never dreamed of. At age twenty-three, I was back from Portland, Oregon. After the sixty-third day of constant downpour, I decided to finally move back home. Four years of enduring depression from the weathered city was enough for me. It was all I could do to jump in my little shitbox of a 1991 Geo Prism and get the fuck out of dodge.

I followed my boyfriend, Chase, out west to find a fresh new life when I was eighteen. Chase had a job already lined up and I wanted to travel the country with him. What people didn't know was I really wanted to run away. Running to a new place and meet new people who didn't know anything about me or my past was enticing. I like strangers, and there are a lot of them in the world. I can be anyone I want to be with strangers. I can be fun and generous. I can be moody and negative. Strangers never saw all sides of me. Portland, Oregon was the right place to go as it was the furthest state from the east coast, where family and high school friends watched me go through ups and downs that didn't always shine a bright light on me. But five years later, that light dimmed on me once more when Chase and I broke up.

I tried to make him see that five years of playing house was enough time for us to be a forever couple. He didn't see it that way and so I broke all the commitment rules. I hung around for several months after the breakup to see if anything changed. When nothing did, I saw no reason to stay in Portland. It was my fault, of course. I didn't want any more from that city. I didn't want to meet new strangers anymore. I got bored. So, running back home was damn good plan and I was prepared to reinvent myself in my hometown and meet new strangers. Again.

I get bored pretty fast with just about every person, every place, and everything. When I was thirteen, I bought an impressive horoscope book and created astrology charts for all my friends. Of course, I did mine and was astonished to read that, as an Aquarian in sun position and a Leo in moon position, I would never settle down. I was a creative and carefree person, it said. I didn't want to believe the predictions, but as life went on, I realized that I was the indifferent girl that the chart portrayed me to be. I always felt like a drifter. I went with my own flow. Most would say I belonged on Shakedown Street at a Phish concert because I'm a tree hugging, crunchy hippie. I didn't bother with makeup or primping for guys. I was audacious and found normalcy mundane.

A friend once described me as a resilient and incredible woman. I could see why she would say that. I appeared that way on the outside but it was still difficult to swallow that compliment because it simply wasn't true. Low self esteem was engrained into the very core of my being, although outward appearances convinced everyone else otherwise. The heartwarming thank you I replied with was plastic. I attempted many times to become someone that I could love. Alas, being outspoken and defensive found me in predicaments that required mending. Mending the fuck ups in life took much more time than working towards life goals. Therefore, I stuck to what I knew made me *feel* better. Partying seemed to be the only way to escape the reality of my life.

The outward beauty of my past boyfriends had never been important unless I felt a deep emotional connection to the guy. Once I saw their inner luster, that's when they became hopelessly beautiful. My friends would probably say that is also a bunch of bullshit because I typically date tall bad boys. Regardless of who I was with, in the end, I always drove relationships away with my drinking. I liked to drink, and when I did, the alcohol convinced me that I was the most beautiful person in the room. I became the life of the party and people gravitated to my many stories of drifting uninhibited through life. Even in high school, I found smoking pot in the parking lot to be a better living experience than sitting through my history class. I lived in the moment, and when shit got tough, it was time to move on.

Chase was a solid, dependable guy with a steady job, a great apartment and a lot of patience for my outlandish behavior. He didn't really know who I was, but after all, I didn't either. Despite our break up, we remained friends. I didn't want to disrespect the five years between us even though it all went to hell. Many of our mutual friends didn't understand me. I soon realized that he and I were polar opposites, even if we had five years under our belts. After Chase and I broke up, I could tell that people wanted to say something but didn't. They all exchanged glances when we spoke amicably at the bars. They were probably muttering that I was a big dumbass for letting a well-established, constant guy in my life go. I didn't agree. I no longer felt anything passionate for him or our future. Chase understood the reason I needed to leave town. He didn't want to go down the path I had insisted for so long and couldn't deter me from my ultimatum. Besides, we were friends more than anything. Fortunately, Chase didn't grovel. I think he was more desolate about being alone.

Chase insisted on helping me drive to Boulder, Colorado where an old friend, Eve, would help me continue my journey back to the east coast. Eve was three years older than me but we knew each other from the soccer days in high school. She was one person I could talk to about *anything* because I looked up to her like a sister. She was my rock during the high school years. I called her at anytime, day or night, to vent about what was going on at home and in school. I took the T into the city many weekends when she was at Boston University. We had regular coffee dates and I helped her through a really painful break up during her sophomore year. We never had to ask for help from one another. It was a given that if one of us called, we were there for the other one. Sadly, we grew apart after she took a job in Colorado so this road trip with her was a really special reunion.

Chase and I were amicable during the first leg of our trip. He laughed about old memories as I cringed about all that time lost. With a heartfelt goodbye and good luck at the Denver airport, I felt weightless as I walked through the automatic doors to the Geo Prism of my future. The sun was shining. There was no more rain. The depression was lifting, outside and in. Eve brightened the rest of the trip by bringing up old stories of soccer, parties and guys. We laughed all night like sisters in the hotels and ate local food across the nation. She didn't have to ask a lot of questions to understand me. I admired her as a person and would always be there for her with arms wide open. Before we parted at Logan Airport, she reminded me that I could run to Colorado if Boston didn't work out. I laughed and she raised her eyebrows at me before blowing a kiss and turning towards her gate.

Darcy pulled me out of my reflective thoughts.

"Shit, this song again!" said Darcy as she punched the buttons of the radio, ridding the full blare of Britney's "Oops, I did it again" and settled on Third Eye Blind's "How's it going to be." We instantly fell into song and I smiled at my brother's girlfriend on the first weekend following her 21st birthday.

Darcy was a force of nature. She was beautiful, blonde and a social butterfly. Even when she wasn't drinking, she was everything I wasn't. The moment I got home, I knew what Conner saw in her. She was a high powered magnet. Strong and steady with a sizzle that attracted all men. I was envious of her. She had a great job as an assistant to a fashion designer. She had the true inner confidence I had always desired.

"Where's it going to be?" I asked, pushing the thought of my sad self esteem out of my mind. I told myself that I was out with Darcy tonight and I needed to stay in the moment.

"What? The Greatest Bar didn't satisfy your blood thirst for Boston nightlife?" she asked wryly.

"Oh, come on," I groaned, giving her a sideways glance. "The Greatest Bar isn't so appealing when you spend seven dollars on possibly one of the worst mango margarita in the history of the world. But watching a guy being hauled on a stretcher because he probably spent over three hundred dollars getting so stinking drunk, in fact, was very entertaining."

"It's a classic place to expose you into the Boston nightlife," she said, looking at the sides of her high pumps.

"Yeah… classic," I murmured. I desperately wanted a Portland dive bar with cheap drafts and darts. I loved how I could show up in my pajamas at six pm, not feeling a bit self conscious of how I looked. Guys still hit on me even in my butterfly pajama pants. Tonight, Darcy had spent, and I kid you not, over two hours making my hair straight then curly then straight again. She used hair products that I knew cost more than the gas money it took to drive all the way back to Massachusetts. I felt like a sham in this outfit and makeup. She insisted I looked hot enough to get at least three phone numbers from college boys for a summer roll in the sack. When I laughed at her and told her she was ridiculous, she shot me a look like I shouldn't mess with her opinion. Did she see something about me that I couldn't? Maybe makeup and expensive clothes were the necessaries of my future. I pondered that for a moment before shaking the thought out of my head. *No way.*

Two

Mary Ann's

Bar hopping in Boston can be a daunting task if one wants to experience the city's diversity. It is the exact opposite of the Las Vegas Strip, where every person's desire and comfort can be satisfied on one convenient block. In Boston, nightlife is much more spread out. There is the Cambridge art crowd, the Harvard lounges, and the Southie native bars. None of these are within walking distance, so once you make up your mind about which part of the expansive city you want to be in, you choose from whatever is around. After taking in three bars on Commonwealth Avenue, Darcy clearly looked weary. Because I was the designated driver, I resignedly took control of the evening decisions after she started slurring her words at The Greatest Bar. Men complimented her beauty incessantly and reminded her that she could be straight out of a modeling magazine. I rolled my eyes and told her to hand over the keys as I asked for a diet Coke from the bartender.

"No booze tonight, baby?" he asked in the thickest Boston accent I had yet to hear since I got home. It still took me aback, hearing that sexy drawl. It was hot, even though this particular guy was not my type at all. Muscular gym guys in black shirts never really did it for me, but the Irish Celtic knot tattooed on his forearm did catch my attention and I smiled.

I took a deep breath and said the worst sentence known to man. "Nope, I'm the designated driver," I replied.

"Ah, DD! It takes an extraordinary woman to refrain from my alcoholic drinks," he said, winking at me as he placed both of his palms on the mahogany bar.

He looked me over, rather suggestively, and told me DD drinks were on the house. He stopped his examination of my body when he stopped on my BeBe crop top and the barely there cleavage. After a pause, he sighed and walked off when he was motioned by another patron. Darcy had insisted I show off her Tiffany necklace to accentuate the gaudy getup, making me look like a Boston rich girl, even though I only had two hundred dollars in my bank account. *Ugh.* I threw two dollars on the bar and walked away.

Darcy downed two more drinks and that sent me over the edge. A thirty something man was trying to get her to sit on his lap. Suddenly, the plush brown couch with mahogany siding didn't look so classy. The guy looked like he had just gotten out of his cramped cubicle job at some elite financial firm in the district. Disgusted with the live images in front of me and the ever growing sham of the evening, I pulled Darcy off the couch and told her it was time to go. She protested just as much as the white collared jackass. Jesus, he wasn't even beer goggle worthy. As she continued to complain, I swear I heard murmurs from the guy behind her, saying that I was a rich prude. *That was the funniest line of the evening. Looks can be so deceiving.*

Sighing with impatience, I glared over her shoulder to get the guy to stop staring at Darcy's ass. I firmly put my hands on her wobbling shoulders and appeased her with a warm reply.

"Okay. One more bar but no inappropriate groping this time," I laughed. "You are such a silly drunk, but you are a one hot lady."

My brother would be pissed the next morning and expecting a full report about the entire night's events. Because he had been an uncharacteristically possessive boyfriend lately, Conner didn't encourage our plans to celebrate Darcy's 21st in girl style. There was a lot of clenched fists and eye rolling on his part. Darcy finally convinced him that the night out was actually for my benefit since I just returned to the one of the greatest city for nightlife. Conner was finishing up his last semester of his senior year at Boston College with high honors. He would be going on a small tour with his band "The O'Malley Band" this summer. He was the lead singer and guitarist and could drink them down with the best of them. He chose to celebrate Darcy's birthday romantically alone after his college finals were over. Now that was typical Conner. His scholastic and musical goals always came first. Girls were a very distant second but there was something about Darcy that he was very protective of. He was a bit overbearing with Darcy but I hadn't seen him with a girlfriend in years so what did I know? Since I had been in the northwest for the past five years, I didn't understand this new side to Conner. Maybe Darcy was the one for him.

I sat behind the wheel of the Benz and it felt so foreign to my tin box Prism. I pulled back the seat to accommodate my 5'6" height as opposed to Darcy's 5'1" when she scared the living hell out of me and shrilled, "On to Mary Ann's!!! It's the ultimate rite of passage to Boston's nightlife."

"Okay," I sighed, as she pointed me to the one way streets that would get us back onto Commonwealth Avenue towards Chestnut Hill.

While looking for a free parking spot on a side street, I ignored Darcy's compliments of how beautiful I looked and what fun it would be to surround me with Boston College boys at Mary Ann's. It was such bullshit. I knew without a doubt that she was having a great time so I simply smiled at her. I efficiently paralleled parked in a spot near the large, yellow neon sign that read, "Mary Ann's." It was part of a small older strip mall and it wasn't what I expected from Darcy and all of her elegant, debonair places. The previous three bars were set in quiet and upscale locales. Mary Ann's was their polar opposite. It sat on the corner of the Cleveland Circle hot spot, where the homeless ask for change and the Dunkin Donuts had a line spilling out on the sidewalk. I fidgeted with my clutch, pulling out my ID and money for the cover. The bouncer looked me straight in the eyes and back down at the ID then said in a gruff voice, "No covah, go on." He looked over my head and checked out Darcy's driver's license *and* her breasts. Darcy breezed past me as I stopped in the middle of the door and took in the infamous Mary Ann's. Holy shit, this place reeked of testosterone and beer. It was a cross of a Southie Pub and a college bar. I was stunned speechless.

The bar had three levels with crowded tables and large open spaces, but was still packed with loud conversation and laughter. The main bar was a large, wooden, and fairly worn down square directly to my left. The chairs around it were surrounded by guys with Red Sox hats and Boston College tee shirts. Darcy had already noticed a few of Conner's friends on the first level in the back and told me to get her a beer before heading toward the swarm of people in the dart area. *Ugh.* I already felt the stench of alcohol and sweat rising up the back of my neck. I continued to the bar, trying to inch my way in between two guys that were sitting and laughing at a boisterous blonde behind them as she was slurring her words. All of a sudden, I felt a panic attack coming on. A crowd of drunken strangers in an enclosed place was just not my idea of a great time. This was a far cry from The Greatest Bar, where leather seats were mostly vacant by design, and one person could sit and people-watch the night away. I felt like I was in the middle of a Beastie Boys mosh pit, although "Don't Stop Believin" by Journey blared through the jukebox. As I was pushed backed from the bar, I stood dumbstruck at how to proceed to the bar without yelling some obscenities at the rowdy, cocky college boys. My BeBe shirt certainly didn't do the trick at Mary Ann's. I scanned the room for Darcy to assist me with getting her drink but all I saw were blonde girls with large breasts and legs that went forever. I felt twenty years older than everyone in the room even though I was probably only a year or two older.

Why did I come here again? Darcy said it was a rite of passage. A passage to where? I stood, fingering the Tiffany necklace, and wondered who the hell I was trying to impress. How did I get to the place in my life? More specifically, how did I get to this shitty bar? Thoughts of Chase and the downpour rain made me long for the comforts of my pajama bottoms and the slot machines at the neighborhood bar back in Portland.

When I slowly lifted my eyes, I was startled to see a guy towering over me with a large grin on his face. He was tall with dark brown hair that covered his ears but was mussed up from a recent shower. He wore a blue and white striped rugby shirt with an Irish emblem on the left side that displayed his perfectly chiseled arms. They were so tan and oh so yummy. This guy was most definitely my type, appearance wise obviously. He continued to smile at me as his eyes warmed over my face, like he was trying to memorize my features. He was the most attractive guy I had seen the entire night.

"Hello," he yelled over the music. He had a tinge of an accent that I couldn't quite place. *English? Scottish?*

"Hi," I replied, licking my lips in anticipation of an upcoming conversation.

He faced the bar and sighed. "Not getting a pint in this bar anytime soon." He rubbed his chin with his large hand as I downright stared at him.

Irish. He was a sexy Irishman.

"I've been waiting fifteen minutes," I said as I looked around again for Darcy, hoping that someone already got her a drink. I hated being DD and her waitress to boot. This night was a total bad call on my part. The tall, yummy guy caught me looking around and could see my apprehension. He turned my chin back to him and gave me a sweet smile. All my worry about Darcy dissolved in that moment.

"Hmmm," he said. "Let me see if I can give it a go." He stepped up between the two guys talking to the blonde, and with the sexiest Irish accent I had ever heard, he ordered six Guinness drafts. Everyone turned to look at him and their mouths dropped open. Even the female bartender paused for a moment before heading to the beer taps. I smiled to myself and my cheeks reddened when he looked back to me and winked. Throwing down bills, he turned to me and said, "Cian. Cian Murphy." After staring at him silent for what seemed like an hour, he stood up straight and turned back to the bar. He just introduced himself and I couldn't find my tongue. *Nice, Lizzie.* Cian looked perplexed as he looked down at the six tall glasses of thick, black liquid before he sent me a pleading look. "Can you help me bring these to me lads over there?" He pointed to the right of the bar.

"You're joking, right?" He wanted me to be his waitress, too? I should just throw on an apron and start making money off this night.

He quirked his lips into a smile and asked, "What? You don't think I have lads waiting for their pints?"

"No, no…" I stammered. "Your accent. Does it get you what you want all the time?"

He looked at me puzzled for a moment and then leaned forward so we were nose to nose. "Is the accent working on you?" he asked with a sly smile.

"Yeah right." I rolled my eyes. "But… it is a hell of a good way to make people notice you and get you pints when needed," I replied with air quotes around the word pints. My night was becoming more interesting because of this chance meeting. I was feeling flirty and listening to Cian talk softly into my ear all night would be exquisite. He laughed out loud at my banter and nudged me towards the glasses then cocked his head to the right.

I followed him on his heels to avoid being separated and nearly stumbled around three guys sucking on the necks of busty college girls. I paused in awe. Those girls had somehow managed to pull their shirts up into the Maryanne crop style. Cian surprisingly didn't look their way but only glanced back at me. He was probably trying to make sure I didn't drop the two beers I carried all over the floor. I was not the type of girl that belonged in this bar but Cian didn't seem to notice.

Cian and I stepped up to the worn leather, circular booth where four guys were very boisterous. Cian nodded to them. "Lads, this is…shit, I didn't ask your name," he said with a grin. The other guys laughed at him and looked at me expectantly.

"Yeah, sorry. I didn't offer it either. Elizabeth. Lizzie… Lizzie O'Malley," I said as my face started to redden. *Why was I suddenly embarrassed?*

"Ah, an Irish transplant," one of the blond haired guys from the back of the booth said with a thick Irish accent of his own. I didn't exactly know what that meant. Was it because of my last name? My freckles? My red hair? Yes, I was part Irish. I was also part Scottish, Canadian French, and surely something else. But really, after generations of mutt reproduction, I was just American. It was that simple.

Cian put all the drinks in front of the guys, and I started to say something else but nothing came to mind. What was I going to say? These guys were a bunch of fucking hotties with their Irish accents, and amazingly, the booth was far, far away from the torturous mosh pit of grimy sweat. Cian turned and handed me the last Guinness.

"Oh, no, thanks," I said. "I'm the designated driver tonight. I'm not drinking."

They all stared at me like I was making a joke and waited for me to take back my declaration. One of them started laughing and asked, "DD? For who?" while squinting his brown eyes up to me. He looked as hammered as Darcy did the last time I saw her. When was that? Like an hour ago?

"Uh-huh. For a friend that I believe I've lost to this place." I turned around, faking to really care if I saw her. I wanted to sit with these guys, but tried to act disinterested.

Cian put his arm around my shoulder and nudged me to sit while shoving the Guinness into my hand. He sat down next to me, sticking me smack in the middle of him and an equally cute blond guy, who was immersed in his own conversation with the others. I don't even think he noticed I was there. It didn't matter because all I felt was the sensation of being so close to Cian. His leg was practically straddling mine under the table. Perhaps I wasn't leaving him enough room? His legs were pretty long. The group of guys continued their conversation over some rugby match they had played that afternoon when Cian whispered in my ear, "I'm glad you finally got your pint."

14

I gave him a coy smile. He smiled back then joined the group, still talking about sports. *Fucking yawn.* At least it could have been about American football.

Moments passed and I suddenly felt like the foreigner. In my own city, no less. Well, shit. If I was going to be packed in the middle of unique testosterone, I was going to play my hand at the estrogen. Wake up, woman and turn on the charm

"What the hell are you guys talking about?" I said loudly. I felt downright stupid, sitting in the middle of five guys arguing over rugby with Irish fucking accents.

They all turned to stare at me…again. Jesus, could this night get any worse? It was a night of pompous financial men, guys on stretchers, idiotic Boston College guys drunkenly territorial and now this. Here was an Irish guy named Cian, who was apparently trying to make a move on the poor girl that couldn't get her own damn drink after fifteen minutes. Why was I squeezed in the middle of this booth? This was not my comfort zone, nor was it what I was looking for all night. I wanted one on one interaction with a guy. I wanted to dance and laugh. I didn't want to be ignored anymore. I never would have done this in Oregon. I missed people who I knew well enough to get me out of situations like this one.

I sat back and watched them all talk and laugh once more and sipped on my beer. I was totally uncomfortable. Or was I? I decided to chipper up and flip the switch on my mood. I was, after all, in need of attention since Darcy seemed to suck all of it out of the city of Boston.

"You guys are all wicked smart with your accents and rugby talk. Obviously, this is a college bar but if you think your charming accents are going to get you into those ladies' panties, you're way off. You should be wearing Red Sox hats and perhaps take off the sexy Irish shirts." I said in a rush, quirking my eyebrow up to them.

Laughter rang all around the table. I was starting to feel proud of myself just as a huge crash came from the bar. A girl, lying on the bar, started yelling at a patron who obviously didn't like the body shot he was giving her. Cian and three of his friends from the opposite side of the booth stood up abruptly and headed towards the commotion.

I stared down at my nearly full beer, not realizing the blond on my right was still in the booth with me. I tucked my hair behind my right ear and swallowed the whole pint of Guinness in several solid gulps. Just then, I realized the lone blond guy was staring at me with a wide smile on his face. I shifted in my seat and started to slide out of the booth. He grabbed my hand, and I was jerked back into my seat. I was so shocked by his touch that I couldn't move my body. Literally, my body was battling with my mind so I stayed there, stalk still in the seat. After a few moments of my mind racing for what to do next, one thought took over and everything else fell away. *Stay. He is yours.*

Three

Darts and Driving

I turned to the blond and he inched his nearly full pint of Guinness to me. "Thirsty?" he asked.

"Not really," I said, looking into the bluest eyes I'd ever seen in all my life. They were devastatingly blue. His smile was plastered on and he had the straightest teeth in the room.

"So, Cian?" I furrowed my brow at his abrupt departure from the table.

"Yes, Cian, a close friend and a good lad," he said in an equally thick accent.

"I found him at the bar," I said in a rush. "My friend obviously ditched me and I guess he took pity on me."

"No. He was just being polite. Not all Irishmen are assholes." He chuckled as he took a swill off of one of his other friends' beers and looked back to me. "Cian has a lady back home in Cork. We all go to university there together." Okay, either Cian was sending mixed signals or I didn't understand flirting anymore. Either way, it was time to back off Cian. *Good to know.*

"Why are you here? I mean, not in this dump of a bar, but in Boston?" I asked as I felt the warm rush of Guinness settling into my stomach.

"I'm Teagan," he said as he stuck out his hand.

I shook it and slowly. "Teagan." I sounded it out in like four syllables as I drew it out. He nodded, expressionless.

"I haven't ever met a Teagan," I said with a smirk.

"Well, there you go. Now you have," he replied, taking another swig.

My eyes shifted over to the bar while searching for anything to say in that awkward moment when casual hellos turn into blank space. I wanted to crowd our conversation. It was tough to tell if Teagan wanted the latter, so I gave him an out.

"I guess I should let you up so you see the show at the bar. You wouldn't want to miss a Bahston love squat," I said in the dry accent.

"Good here, thanks, unless you're interested in checking it out," he replied as he looked over me to see his friends at the bar. A delicate touch of his fingers danced across my hand in my lap. I was so shocked at that blatant touch that I turned to face him instinctively.

That's when I was able to take him all in. He wore a red and white striped rugby shirt with another undecipherable emblem on his left chest and khaki pants. I couldn't see his sneakers but I assumed they were European. Sexy. My heart fluttered a bit. He glanced at me and I took two more swigs of my beer, not remembering I was supposed to be the DD. Darcy was far, far away from my thoughts at that point.

I turned to face him with one of my legs crossed in front of me to create space between us.

"So, Teagan, tell me...You didn't answer me. Why are you here with your friends in Boston?" I asked, looking pointedly into his eyes.

Teagan shrugged. "University Cork has a work program that all seniors need to complete. There were many places to choose from." He counted off on his fingers. "Paris, London, China. Since we're all good friends, we took a vote and, well, we chose America. I like technical engineering so I'm officially starting to work at Foster, Brown, and Crass on Monday."

"Do you get paid?" I asked, taking another drink.

He laughed softly and nodded his head.

"Sorry, that was so rude," I said with a frown. "It just sounds like an internship to me. You know, work credits for your degree."

"Don't worry. People ask us that a lot," he replied, waving his hand in the air dismissively.

We sat in silence for a long time. I slowly moved my body away from the intimate position with Teagan as I began to look out over the crowd. It was much rowdier than before and I started to really wonder where the other guys had gone off to. I became restless about how alone I felt and I shivered with the thought. Like he was reading my mind, or my body, Teagan grabbed my hand and said, "Come on, let's play a game of darts and get another pint."

Before I could refuse, I was pushed out of the booth. He maneuvered his body to take the lead up to the bar. He gripped onto my hand and squeezed it firmer than I liked. Teagan pulled me back out into the bar and didn't look back at me to see if I was even okay about that tailspin move. He spotted one of the male bartenders and put up two fingers. Were all Irish guys this dominating? Cian had a girlfriend back in Ireland, yet it felt like he was coming onto me. Was Teagan just taking care of me now, too? Teagan could probably charm the hell out of every girl in this bar just by opening his mouth but I still couldn't read him. His death grip was an obvious sign that there was probably no girl back home waiting for him.

After retrieving the pints from the bartender, he rounded on me. Nose to nose, he placed the glass in my hand. "Here you are, Lizzie O'Malley." His smile was so genuine that I smiled brightly back and thanked him seductively. I felt like I was the only girl in this crowded bar of college bombshells that he was looking at, and I felt more beautiful than anyone else. He wasn't as classically gorgeous as Cian and he wasn't someone I would normally stare after in a mall or on the T, but he looked at me in a way that I'd never experienced in my entire life. His deep penetrating gaze was beautiful and the magnetism between our stares made my stomach flutter. I hadn't felt that flutter in years.

In that moment, I realized that he was not only stunning but mesmerizing. His gaze never left my eyes. To boot, he didn't look drunk, like he wanted to just hook up. He looked like he was really happy to see me, like we were old friends and hadn't seen each other in years. There were no words or tension. It wasn't weird. It just felt right. Was I…was I attracted to this guy?

While we waited to play darts, we had easy conversation, and I relaxed for the first time the whole evening. Teagan and I played three games of darts and laughed at the fact that I was kicking his ass. He startled me when he put his hand on the small of my back and said, "I think it's time to find the lads." I nodded, thinking I would agree to do anything and everything he suggested to me at that point. As we walked back to the table, Darcy cut us off and slurred, "Lizzie, let's go. I just called Conner and he's pissed that I'm so drunk."

20

I looked at her, dumbstruck, and then turned to Teagan. I gave him a sheepish smile, and figured introductions were in order. I really didn't want to leave so I prolonged the moment.

"Darcy, this is Teagan. Teagan, this is Darcy, my brother's girlfriend," I said with fake enthusiasm. I wanted Darcy to see that I did meet a guy that she had insisted on. I also wanted Teagan to know that I wasn't interested in leaving him at all. "Darcy, I'm so sorry but I started drinking by peer pressure." I pointedly looked at Teagan. He laughed out loud and gave me a look that said I was such a liar. I smiled, not paying attention to Darcy as I momentarily got lost in the fact that Teagan and I already had unspoken conversational skills. I turned back to Darcy. "I can't drive yet. Give me another hour or so, okay?"

"No!" Darcy shot back at me, startling me out of my revelation about Teagan. "Your brother is going to dump me. He is so pissed. We have to go now!" She grabbed my hand and practically ran out the crowded door. I left Teagan standing there, already feeling bereft and wishing I had gotten his number. It was the only number I wanted out of Darcy's promised three and I would have used it. The evening sucked once again.

As we headed out to the slightly cooler air on Commonwealth, I turned and faced Darcy. "Honey, I can't drive yet. I'm going to wait in the line for a coffee," I said in my most soothing voice, pointing at Dunkin Donuts." I knew how to coddle drunken friends that want to drive home. My mantra is, "Always keep them from the keys and the car." Keys, check. Car, check. But I knew Darcy always got what she wanted, and I felt uneasy about this. I did feel bad that I drank but I did not feel bad about drinking with the yummy Irishmen. I wasn't shitfaced. I just needed a little time. Nonetheless, I was taken over by guilt that I hadn't been a proper designated driver. It felt like we had only been in Mary Ann's for an hour. Looking down at my watch, I saw it was still so early in the evening that I could get a cup of coffee and wait out the beers I had drunk. Concurrently, I felt awful that I didn't get Teagan's fucking phone number. Ugh. I was so confused.

"No, Lizzie. I…" she stuttered as she tried to put her hands on her hips.

Our conversation was cut off by an Irish accented male yelling, "Lizzie!" I whirled around and saw Teagan step out of Mary Ann's with the boys right on his heels. He looked worried but I thought I saw relief in his expression as our eyes met. I held up my hand to Darcy, silently telling her to wait. I walked towards Teagan.

"Hey, what's going on with your friend?" he asked as he looked over my shoulder and gave a quick cork of his head.

"She wants to go home. We live in Wellesley. It's about 20 miles from here," I said as I pointed up aimlessly to Route 9. "But I…I had three or four beers, I mean, pints and I'm not sure I can drive yet." I frowned in despair. In that moment, those quick twenty miles felt like two hundred to me. I was simply not ready to get behind the wheel. Even the thought of it sent me into a panic attack.

"Aye, I see," he said, smiling at me. He saw the apprehension in my body language and our eyes locked again and I told him it wasn't a joke with my look. His smile sobered and he cleared his throat and looked between Darcy and me.

"Well, our place is right there," he said, pointing over to a big brownstone with a green awning. "She can use the phone to call your brother. I'm sure we can work it out," he said.

22

I pondered his invitation for a moment as I stared deeper into his eyes. All I saw was warmth, and was that...interest? Did he want me to stay with him a little longer? Was this the polite Irishmen gesture that he was talking about in the bar? Why am I even considering this? Darcy couldn't go to the apartment of five foreign bachelors. Conner would flip. He knew about my one-night stands in the past and probably thought I would rub off my promiscuity on Darcy. Whether or not I moved back to Boston to get my head on straight, he obviously didn't trust me. I was at a proverbial fork in the road, where I either made the right choice or the smart choice. I just couldn't figure out which was which.

I looked over my shoulder at Darcy. She was wringing her hands frantically and pacing back and forth on the sidewalk. I walked up to her with determination and put both my hands on her shoulders. "Darcy, these nice guys have a phone right across the street and we need to sober up for just a little while before we go home. Conner isn't going to be mad at you. He will only be mad that I drank tonight. I'll call him myself. It was my bad," I said.

Darcy went absolutely ape shit. Faster than I could think the next word in my head, she shoved my hands off her shoulders and tore my clutch out of my hand with a look of disgust. I was so taken aback by her flailing that I didn't comprehend what was happening until she tore the keys out and was halfway across the street to the car.

"Darcy! Wait! What the fuck are you doing?" I yelled after her. She was stumbling, and for the first time ever, she didn't look so elegant. It was obvious that the drunk driving pep talk wouldn't work on her so forceful intervention was in order. I tried to walk in my heels with grace but the blisters on my feet were popped and holy fuck, it was so painful. I made it to the car as she started to open the door. I threw all my body weight into the door. Fucking ouch! Pain shot up my whole side and I cringed. After several seconds, as she stared at my forceful approach, I regained my composure and got in her face.

"NO!" I angrily said in her face. "You're not going to drive."

"I'm fine." Darcy clipped out each word. I gaped at her and shook my head. Her eyes were glazed over, her mascara not quite crisp and she was swaying just the tiniest bit. Maybe drinking and driving was a normal occurrence, but no one knew more about the consequences than I. By my senior year in high school, five kids were put into the ground after dying at the base of trees. She didn't fully understand that driving drunk was Russian roulette.

Out of the corner of my left eye, I saw the five Irish guys heading towards the car. Cian and one other stood at the front of the car, two took the place behind the car, and Teagan stood next to me. All of them stood at attention, as if they would pick up the car. All they needed was one look from Teagan. He was obviously the alpha leader in the pack.

"Problem?" Teagan asked, looking at Darcy. I felt his words like a sharp knife and knew he was clearly directing the question at me.

Looking down at the ground, and in the smallest voice I could muster, I said, "I was DD. I fucked up. She wants to drive and she has the keys." I balled my fists at my sides and Teagan's eyes were drawn to them. He snapped his head up and blinked twice.

"Damn straight, I'm going to drive!" Darcy slurred out her words. "Now get in, Lizzie. You don't even know these guys." That was very true, but God, I didn't want to get in that car with her either. My head was swimming with alcohol and confusion.

I was swallowed hard as I was overwhelmed by the biggest rush of indecision. How the fuck did I get into this situation? I looked for any alternate choices. Just then, the Green T went whirling by. "We'll take the Green line home and we'll call Conner to get us," I pleaded hopefully.

Darcy smirked at me like I was stupid to even think about it. "I'm fine," she said again, without attitude this time.

"Darcy," I groaned. "I can't drive. I can't let you drive and if you choose to drive, I can't get in that car with you," I said with a pleading glance to Teagan. Turning to him, I asked, "What time is it? There may be one more C line back to Wellesley."

One of the guys at the front crossed his arms over his chest and in a bored voice said, "It's too late. That was the last train."

"Shit," I said under my breath as I rolled my eyes up to Darcy.

"Fine," she said. "You aren't coming. That's fine. I'll see you tomorrow. I need to get to Conner. He's pissed and I need to fix this." She started to fumbled with the car door and keys again, looking flustered

Again, I used all my physical energy and shoved my body back into her car door. I know I left a dent. I tried, without grace, to remove the keys from her hands but she was a spitfire crazed woman on a mission and I couldn't get them pried out of her hands.

One of the guys stepped up and tried to help me talk to Darcy but she just shoved them away. Eventually, they just stood there dumbstruck. Before I could figure out a way to get the keys away from her again, Darcy wedged her body through the tiniest slit of the driver's door. She started the ignition, turned on the headlights and yelled for everyone to move. My shoulders slumped in defeat. After making a several point turn to maneuver her way out of the spot, she was gone. I sat on the curb and threw my head in my hands. *Jesus H. Christ. What have I done this time?*

Four

Couch

I remained hunched over my knees for a long after Darcy drove away. I looked down at my digital Swatch and realized she had to be home by then. I let out a deep exhale, praying that she was safe and making her apologies to my brother. That was not a place where I wanted to be a fly on the wall. Conner was going to be so pissed at me the next day. I didn't even realize Teagan and the rest of them were still there when a taxi cab honked his horn at another car crossing the lane. I felt so alone in my thoughts while the bustling street came to a dead silence. Teagan stayed perfectly still, staring at me while he murmured with one of his friends. He must have been thinking I was having a mental breakdown. People don't just sit on curbs of Boston streets and stare off in space unless something is seriously wrong with them.

I tried to compose myself and rectify any feelings they must have had about me. I cleared my dry throat. "I don't know what to do," I said quietly. "I can take a taxi but that will cost me fifty dollars and I only have a few bucks left on my debit card. Maybe…" I trailed off, looking into my pocket to see if I had brought one of my many credit cards. I knew one of Conner's friends lived nearby. Maybe it was up towards Boston Colleg? But what would I say to him? I couldn't show up at a stranger's house in the middle of the night and plead to sleep on his couch.

Noticing that I was quickly becoming immersed in my thoughts again, Teagan cleared his throat. I looked up to his sweet blue eyes and he held out his hand to me.

"Come on," he said with confidence. "We won't bite you. You can stay on the couch and take the train home tomorrow. Maybe Darcy can pick you up and you can talk then?"

I got to my feet and thanked him in the quietest voice I could muster. I laughed to myself that I was actually going to a stranger's house and pleading with them to let me sleep on their couch. Ten paces down Commonwealth, I said, "I couldn't get in the car. Not like that."

And I couldn't. When I was sixteen, my parents bought me a brand new Nissan because I passed the driving test on the first try. I've always been persistent in my independence, so I practiced for weeks, and just like that, I was on my own way to do as I pleased. One night in June 1993, I was named the designated driver by a bunch of my girlfriends who wanted to go to a keg party. I was quickly distracted by Chase. At that time, he and I had only known each other through mutual friends but we started talking and decided to have a conversation away from the loud Metallica music and keg stands. We stayed in the back of his truck bed and drank his beers, laughing at all the stupid drama at the party. For example, someone thought it was funny to throw tires on the bonfire. By the time we left, I was aware that I had a few beers in me, but I didn't feel intoxicated by any means. After dropping the first two girls off at home, my last girlfriend, Mel, and I decided that we needed snacks. I headed into the 7-11 to get some donuts. When I returned to the car, I found my friend passed out, my car still running and an officer rummaging through my backseat, finding empty beer bottles. I was immediately arrested. Three hours later, my mother bailed me out jail with my donuts in a plastic bag and soot from the burning tires all over my face. I swore to myself, and the judge who suspended my license for a year, that I would never drive drunk again. That year was miserable but I didn't worry about drinking and driving since my license was suspended. Instead, I drank. Oh, how I drank.

Teagan gave me a puzzled look like he was trying to understand me. He shook his head. We both kept our eyes on the pavement as we walked down the street to their apartment. I slowed. Teagan stopped. When he turned around, he was smiling his wide, toothy smile and gently intertwined our hands together. It was so warm and comforting, shocks of pleasure swiftly flashed through my stomach. When we got to his stairs, I was exhausted. I didn't want to be social. I wanted to be alone. Well, that wasn't the whole truth. Teagan could stay with me since his hand was permanently attached to mine and I didn't want to let go.

"Do you mind if I come in…in a little while?" I asked him.

"No, not all," he said. "Let me check on the boys and I'll be right back out." He held up his hands, silently telling me not to go anywhere. It was adorable.

As I sat perched on the steps at 1529 Commonwealth Avenue, I watched drunken college students bound down the street, falling over themselves and laughing. I studied an older lady walking by with a supermarket cart filled to the brim with her prized possessions. I gazed across the street as red and white car lights blurred by. I fought back the urge to cry. Maybe it was because I was coming off the adrenaline rush from the evening. Wasn't this the kind of night I was trying to avoid by leaving Oregon? Stupid drinking and drama didn't sit well with me but it sure as hell followed me wherever I went. I needed to stop being a reckless drinker and find something healthier for myself.

I thought being with Chase was a healthy life choice. Chase was safe. The only reckless thing I did with him was running away to Oregon. Looking back, I knew that we were more friends than lovers, just trying to find a new life for ourselves in a new part of the country.

Teagan stepped out on the stairs and the hard click of the door startled me from my internal scrutiny. He held out a Sam Adams bottle, already opened, and sat down next to me with one of his own.

"Not a great night?" he asked, looking out across the street.

I sighed. "I've had worse." A few moments passed in silence as we drank from our bottles. I could feel him becoming antsy. He obviously wanted to talk.

"How old are you?" he asked.

"Twenty-three. How about you?"

"Twenty-two," he said. I nodded my head and stared at him a bit longer than I should have.

"Why are you looking at me like that?" he asked as he pulled off his beer.

"Twenty-two? I don't know," I stammered. "I'm older than you." I laughed feeling like an idiot that I had been caught staring at him. *Good recovery, Lizzie. Just brilliant.*

Teagan smiled and came closer to me on the steps, resting his thigh against mine. The night was getting chilly and my small giggle obviously told him it was okay to inch towards me. I didn't feel drunk, and I definitely didn't feel like I was in danger. I felt like everything was just as it was supposed to be and I didn't want the night to ever end.

After our beers were long gone, my ass started to numb on the concrete so I politely asked if I could use his restroom. I felt so comfortable with Teagan already and the night's events seemed less dramatic and life altering with him on my side. He took my hand, unlocked the front door with a key and proceeded to the left apartment on the first floor. Opening the door, he murmured, "My friends are a little out of control after midnight so consider yourself warned." He gave a teasing nudge to my shoulder, making me stumble into the apartment.

He walked me to the restroom and I locked myself in. I stared at my face and tried to remove the makeup Darcy had plastered on me. I sat down on the covered toilet and listened for any craziness in the apartment. When I first walked in, I saw the kitchen and living area and the right hall went down to the bathroom and two bedrooms. I glanced in one bedroom on my way to the bathroom and saw three mattresses on the floor with hardly any covers and flat pillows.

Pondering where Teagan slept, and hoping I wouldn't sleep on a floor since all of them were twin beds, I heard the boisterous laughter of the guys coming from the living room. Then I remembered there was a couch I could sleep on and I let out a sigh of relief. "Baby Got Back" pounded through a CD player as I tentatively stepped out of the bathroom. Teagan, standing to my right, grabbed my waist and made me gasp. "Jesus Christ, you scared me. What the hell is going on?" I asked.

"I was wondering the same thing," he said in a slow, thick accent. I looked him up and down and marveled at his attentiveness. He was very attractive with his long jaw, high cheeks bones, and strong arms.

"Huh?" I asked, breaking the moment of appreciating him.

"You were in there so long, I thought you passed out. I was about ready to break the door down." He laughed. "Come on. These guys are about to put on an interesting show."

He walked me down the hallway to the living room. Two of the guys were talking on one couch. The other one, I think his name was Aidan, was on another couch, looking up at the last roommate who, and I kid you not, was completely naked except for his briefs and had his ball sack hanging out of the side. Dancing around the wooden coffee table in the middle of the room, he stopped right in front of me and made a indecent gesture with his back. What the hell was I watching? Why does one man in a crowd of guys get totally naked and do this?

"Is he following through on a dare?" I asked as I slipped my eyes from the man's nut sack to Teagan. Teagan was not staring at the guy on the table. He was watching me intently. He was gauging my reaction. After a few minutes, he lifted his shoulders. "Kellen's just like that. He likes to be naked and he loves attention." He made it sound like this was a normal occurrence. Good to know that the Irish are so free with their bodies. I started laughing so hard, I couldn't stop. I hadn't laughed that hard in months and it felt great. I told Teagan I was going to pee my pants.

He replied with a smirk, "I'm not allowing you to go back in the bathroom again, so piss away."

We took seats comfortably close to each other just when Kellen stepped off the table and pronounced he was tired and headed off to bed. Just like that? I guess the show was over. Soon after, Cian and Aidan followed him to their beds. Teagan and I made conversation for about an hour, mostly about Boston, what he had seen so far, and what Oregon was like. It was an easy exchange. His last roommate was still awake and in the living

32

room with us. He had curly, jet black hair with freckles and green eyes. He was beautiful, too! He tried to include himself in our conversation every once in a while but remained stuck to the couch, looking down into his bottle.

I felt a bit uncomfortable by his presence so I held out my hand and said, "Hey, you probably don't remember my name but I'm Lizzie O'Malley." He took my hand gingerly and kissed the back of it and quietly said, "I remember, Lizzie. I am Freddie. Freddie Quinn." He gave me the most adorable smile. Our eyes locked, my stomach plummeted again, and my cheeks flushed. What the fuck was up with adorable and sweet Irish boys? I had always imagined that Irishmen were drunken idiots that crossed their arms over each other and danced the Irish step dance.

I noticed Teagan out of the corner of my eye staring at Freddie and then he cleared his throat.

"Well, I guess I should head to bed. It was a pleasure to meet you, Lizzie," Freddie said with an intense, smoldering look.

I didn't want Freddie to go. I felt an unexplained tightness in my chest with his sudden urge to leave. I wanted to talk to him more. *Ugh, another internal debate.* I hadn't noticed him in all of the drama that night and even though I didn't know him at all, I wasn't ready to be alone with Teagan. There was a short stare down between Freddie and Teagan. Was Teagan demanding that Freddie leave so he could pursue me? Did Freddie want to pursue me, too? I want to ask him to stay a little longer but the moment was gone. He started off the couch and headed to his room in a hurried manner. Just as he rounded the hallway to his twin bed, I stopped him short. "Goodnight, Freddie Quinn. It was so nice to meet you," I said as I took in his long body. So fucking sexy. He looked back at the both of us and faintly grinned.

33

Teagan looked at me strangely at first as he saw the look I gave Freddie and then quickly changed it to smoldering. With hooded lids, he took my cheeks in his hands. He briefly kissed me. I felt a surge of energy rush through my body. I looked up into his deep blue eyes and smiled. His kiss was so soft and tentative. His lips were confident but I could tell he was shaking slightly. I moved my hands over his tight arms and grasped the back of his short blond hair to pull him down to me. He rolled over me and we moved in sync to each other's hands, lips, and bodies.

I basked in his warmth over my body and struggled to get my breath as he consumed me. We never lost any clothes. Strangely, there was something naked about our feverish intimacy. I have never felt so emotionally comforted until then. For once, I felt complete in the arms of another.

Five

Consequences

I woke up the next morning to the blazing sun pouring through the front windows and winced at my extreme hangover. Counting over the amount of drinks I consumed, I couldn't understand why I felt such a throbbing headache. Then, I felt the arms of a shirtless Teagan wrap around me as he sighed into my ragged red hair. His chest was smooth but oh so tight. He was warm and protective. Snapping to attention, I looked down to my body and realized I was fully dressed. Hmm…not a one-night stand. How very unlike me.

"Good morning, American girl," Teagan murmured. I lay back down and let him pull his arms around me.

"Good morning." I sighed. Relief flooded me when I realized I hadn't exposed my naked body to him. Nonetheles, it had been the most intimate night I'd ever had with a guy. Even Chase had never given me this. He never wanted to cuddle or just kiss me softly and talk. He was an in and out guy and then it was on to the next task at hand.

Last night was like no other I'd ever experienced in my life. Teagan and I stayed up until five am, talking and laughing about his life in Cork County, Ireland, and my grand gestures to travel the world, which already included most of the United States. Around five thirty, our kisses died down and we cuddled until sleep took over. He didn't attempt anything more than feeling down my sides and brushing back my hair. I tried to understand why he didn't want anything more from me. Most guys would have tried to score but not Teagan. I was mystified and knew Teagan was different. Sex didn't matter to him. I was what mattered to him last night as he tried to get to know me. Maybe I had comforted him as much as he comforted me.

He lightly kissed the side of my cheek and pulled me closer. I could hear showers turning on and off and techno music playing in the back bedrooms. I turned to look out to the hall. Freddie was standing inside the living area with one shoulder perched against the wall. With his arms crossed over his blue shirt, he stood there and watched us on the couch. Was he staring at me or us? Teagan looked up and politely said good morning to Freddie before he dropped his head down to kiss the back of my neck. As I sheepishly smiled, I heard Freddie sigh. He went to the kitchen and rummaged through the refrigerator for breakfast items.

"Hurling in an hour," Freddie said over his shoulder to Teagan.

"Is it that late?" Teagan exclaimed. I could tell from his urgent change in body language that he was about to get up, so I beat him to it. I pulled off the small blanket Teagan had retrieved from his room during the night and stood to straighten my shirt.

"Freddie," I said. "Is there a phone here? I need to call my friend, I mean, my brother." Reality set in about the events from the night before and my heart started to pound. I should have punched Darcy in the face to stop her from driving. What the fucking shit was she thinking? Once again, I confirmed that drinking makes all rational thoughts dissipate.

Freddie looked at me, taking in my fully clothed body and nodded his head to the cordless phone lying next to the wall in the kitchen. I turned to Teagan. I felt like I should say something since we spent the whole night snuggled together.

"Teagan, I need to…" I trailed off as I saw the back of his body walking to his bedroom. Okay, I guess the night is officially over.

I turned to take the phone off the hook and caught Freddie gazing at me again. I darted my eyes away. I quickly dialed my home phone and Conner picked up on the second ring.

"Conner," I said hurriedly.

"Where the fuck are you, Liz? What the fucking hell were you thinking last night? Do you know how much I hate you right now?" he screamed into the handset. I had to pull it away from my ear while Freddie looked over at me with concern.

I took the phone into the farthest corner of the living room and slipped down to the ground, resting my head on my knees.

"I know, Conner. I tried to stop her. She said you were going to…" I started to respond. I wanted to tell him my side of the story, since he obviously blamed me for everything even when I had tried desperately to stop her. At least I had tried to stop her. Did I do enough?

He cut me off. "Darcy was in the fucking God damn hospital when I was called by her mother. She had a .23 blood alcohol level. She was fucking arrested last night and totaled the fucking car. What…What… Why the fuck weren't you driving? This is entirely your fault you stupid, selfish…"

I hung up. Shit, I couldn't do it. I didn't want to fight him while my head continued to pound. I wanted him to see my shaking body in person. He would understand better if he knew how much last night affected me, too. She was arrested? *Oh my fucking God.*

I don't know how long I sat against that wall, gripping the phone in my hand. I wished I never called home. I wished I hadn't hung up. Was Darcy in critical condition? Why was she hospitalized? The car was totaled. I couldn't wrap my mind around it and one finger went to my temple to rub out the disaster that would follow. My relationship with my brother was totaled.

Tears poured down over my stupid Bebe cropped shirt and I remembered all the things she said to me the night before. Darcy had repeatedly told me how beautiful I was and how she was so glad I was home again. Bullshit. I just wanted to crawl in a corner. I'm not beautiful. I'm not anything. I am a stupid, selfish girl that runs at any chance to start over and it landed me in the same place over and over and over. Once again, I was in a dark place and needed to feel comforting attention. I needed to get my fucking head on straight. I tried so hard to do the right thing last night and I hadn't. Now I was with five strange men. The really nice and beautiful Teagan would only turn and walk away from me. I knew in that exact moment what to do. Run.

I stood up abruptly, placed the phone on the stand, and grabbed my clutch. When I turned to look at Freddie in the kitchen, all I could do through my tear streaked face was fake a smile. I tore open the door and headed out in the brisk morning air towards Cleveland Circle Station. I heard Freddie's voice calling after me as I crossed over the tracks but I didn't look back. After boarding the train, I sat straight ahead, feeling empty and numb. The swaying of the train did nothing to shake me out of the staleness I felt.

When the T reached the Wellesley stop, I got up slowly and started the three mile walk back to my house. After only a quarter of a mile, I tore off my heels and walked barefoot the rest of the way home. Sleep deprived and red faced, I stopped in front of my door and looked down at my watch. It was just after 1:00pm. No cars in the driveway. No noise from the inside as I put my ear against the door. I quietly opened the heavy, wooden door and crept in.

Conner was sitting on the bottom step of the stairs with his head in his hands. He looked up when he saw me and I saw no tears. He just looked me over and started shaking his head back and forth.

I gave him a sympathetic look and said, "I know what you think about me. I know what I think about me. Just tell me she isn't seriously hurt." My eyes started to tear up and my body started trembling again. I could tell that Conner noticed my trembling hands as I adjusted my clutch under my armpit. He sighed dramatically.

After closely looking at my face, gauging whether or not to tear me a new one, he closed his eyes and said, "She isn't seriously hurt."

"That's it? What happened? How did she get into the accident?" I asked, feeling like he didn't wanted to punish me by not telling me anything.

"Well, she was drunk, Lizzie," he said somberly. I took a deep breath.

"I am so sorry, I know," I whispered. "Please tell me what happened."

"She ran into two guard rails and her car flipped over. It took the Jaws of Life to get her out. She was banged up pretty bad. She was taken to the hospital and then this morning, the cops arrested her," Conner said numbly.

"Is she out? Can I go see her?" I asked.

"No one wants to see you, Lizzie," he said.

I started to cry. Big angry tears and hiccups prevented me from explaining what happened. But it was my fault and no one had to tell me that twice. I would live with the shame for a long time.

I quickly rushed by him, up the stairs and rounded the banister to my room. I quietly closed and locked my door. I tore off my clothes quickly and pulled on the biggest, ugliest tee shirt I could find. I flipped my Sarah McLaughlin CD in my player and lay down in my bed. After long thoughts of what would have happened if I didn't drink last night, I wondered if I cared about what could have happened with Teagan. I slowly closed my eyes and drifted into a dark and deep sleep.

Six

Conversation

I woke up at five thirty in the evening, feeling groggy and dreadful. After staring up at the ceiling, I had a sudden urge to call Darcy to apologize. I didn't know how much she remembered. I went to my cordless phone in the corner and dialed Darcy's number. I wouldn't go near Conner to ask how she was because I knew the conversation would end up with the blame on me. On the third ring, Darcy's mother answered the phone.

"Hi, Mrs. Worthington. Is Darcy there?" I asked, tentatively.

Darcy's mother sighed and I listened for her response. I tensed my hands in my lap and sat straight up. She had to answer me. It was the civil thing to do, and if nothing else, Mrs. Worthington was polite to a fault. She's a polished Wellesley woman. She must've known I was the one that was with her and the one that tried to body block her car…twice. I rubbed my side and knew there had to be one hell of a bruise. But, I did have every right to know what Darcy was feeling towards me and what happened last night.

"Lizzie, now is not a good time. Darcy is sleeping. Perhaps you could call her another time," she murmured.

"Mrs. Worthington, I am so sorry. I don't know how I could possibly make up for what happened but it was my fault and I should have tried harder to stop her from driving. I promise I did everything I could to take the keys and stop…"

The phone clicked off. I set the phone down on the cradle and lay down on the floor before I started to cry quietly again. I

didn't think I would ever be able to make my friendship with
Darcy right. I didn't deserve to be her friend.

As I listened to the murmurs and noises from the rest of
the house, I tried to think of something appropriate to say should
I run into my mom or dad. After pulling it together, trying to pep
talk myself into believing that tomorrow would be a better day, I
tiptoed out to the bathroom. I took a long shower. It felt so good
to clean off the night before. I wanted to wash all the guilt and
shame from my body. After I dried off, I inched the door open to
watch for any signs of my family then dashed to my room. I saw
a tray with a sandwich and a bottle of water next to my closed
door. I picked it up quickly then locked my door. I wanted to lock
out the memories. I wanted to lock out everyone who knew what
happened. I didn't even want to face my mother or father after
another disastrous moment of my life. If I were a little bit
stronger, or less hung over, I may have gone downstairs to face
the music, but no... I decided to hide for as long as I could.

Sunday morning came in lazy. I watched the large oak
tree sway in the breeze through the window next to my bed. I
heard the neighborhood kids playing and riding their bikes. I
watched the lawnmowers and the occasional expensive car
passing by. I turned to look out my front window to my red Geo
Prism on the side of the road. Why am I here? Why did I come
home? Sure, I fucked up in Oregon, too, but at least my family
didn't have front row seats. I could be anonymous there but
here... Everyone knows I'm unfastened and out of control. I
stayed in my room, my only safe place. Watched the scary world
from inside my respite, I prayed the outside wouldn't swallow me
whole the next time I stepped out on the front steps.

By two pm, I was sitting on the floor by the side of my
bed, throwing M&M's at my door. I concentrated on the candies

that were flying through the air. It seemed the green ones always bounced off the door while the brown ones slipped past the one inch space between the door and its frame. I jumped when a knock on my door took me out of the brown, green, and red meditation. It had been twenty four hours since I talked to another soul and I was content to let it stay that way. I stayed silent, hoping that whoever was at the door would just leave.

"Liz, I know you're awake," Conner belted out from the other side of the door, trying to open it.

"What?" I yelled.

"You have a phone call. Some guy, Irish maybe?" he replied.

I started towards my cordless and realized it was dead from being off the hook for so long. I quietly opened the door and stuck my hand out for the phone. Conner handed it to me and looked down at the brown M&Ms and said, "Nice." As I closed the door, I saw him kneel down and pick up some of them then pop them in his mouth. Gross.

I sat back down on the floor and cautiously put the phone to my ear. "Hello?" I answered tentatively.

"Lizzie?"

Teagan.

"Yes? This is she," I replied wearily.

"Ah, so I *did* get the right number," he said with a smile in his voice. It melted my heart and instantly, my numb feeling started to dissipate.

"Hey, Teagan. How did you get my number?" I asked.

"Ah, well, you called this number from my place yesterday before you left," he stated. "Freddie said you looked upset when you left so I thought I would call and see how you are getting on."

"Well…" I sighed, not sure if I really wanted to have this conversation. I paused for a minute. Wait, why is he calling me? Am I excited about this? Is this connection to the latest worst-night-of-my-life going to trigger more days of self-loathing?

"Lizzie?" he asked, sounding concerned.

"Yeah, I'm here. Listen, a lot of crazy shit went down the other night with Darcy and I'm kind of not doing well. I'm not really sure I want to talk about it," I replied.

"Ah. Okay. Well, I was going to call you yesterday but we had practice then we had a concert last night. So…I am calling now."

"Concert?"

"Yeah, David Gray," he said with a chuckle. "He was brilliant."

"Oh yeah, I know him. British, right?" I probed.

"Mmm-hmm. So what are you doing today?" he asked. I paused. Was he asking me out? What in God's name is this? No guy calls the after a night like that. Well, not since Chase.

"I… I… I'm just sitting here throwing M&Ms at my door. It really is quite fascinating," I deadpanned.

"M&M's? Are you eating them as well? Ah, never mind. You have a car, correct? I think I remember you saying that Friday night *or* Saturday morning," he said with innuendo. He obviously wanted to see me. He liked being with me on Friday night.

"Yes. I have my beater, but it got me 3000 miles across the country, so it's safe to say, I have a car," I rambled on, explaining way too much about my car. I already felt the anticipation about seeing Teagan again.

"Can you come over? Maybe we could go for a walk or something," he asked with more persistence.

"Umm. Sure. What time?"

"How about now?"

"Well, I need to take a shower and do some other stuff. How about 3:30?" I glanced in the mirror and realized I had some serious work to do.

"Sounds perfect," he replied. "Oh and Lizzie? I want to give you my phone number in case you have trouble finding the place again."

"It's okay. I have caller ID and I'm writing it down now. Plus, I memorized the steps I sat on for hours that night. I should be fine," I said with a little sarcasm.

"Great. See you later." He hung up.

I sat there, looking at the phone in my hand. I started off the floor and collected all my candies and threw them into the trash. I lit a candle then a cigarette and fell onto my bed. I popped David Gray into my CD player and turned it on full blast.

An hour later, I left a note for my family that I was meeting an old friend for dinner and I would call as soon as I knew my plans. I jumped in my car and headed for Route 9,

straight back to Teagan, a guy that I suddenly had butterflies for.
Our phone call was brief but it was full of something different.
Promising? He explained why it took him a whole day to call
me? Maybe I meant more to him. Oh hell, I was probably just
reading too much into it.

Seven

Walk

When I pulled up to Teagan's place on Commonwealth Avenue, it was clear that all the residents were still going about their lazy Sunday. There was absolutely no parking. With a dreadful sigh, I double parked outside his place and ran up the stairs only to find that I didn't actually remember the apartment number. I hit all the first floor apartment buzzers.

I looked down to my dark Dickies jeans and Counting Crows tee and wondered how different I looked in my normal attire. Would Teagan notice I wasn't wearing expensive clothes and jewelry? My hair was naturally pulled back in a wet, messy bun. Long hair was usually my preference but I always pulled it back to keep the front locks out of my eyes. I loathed my thick red hair when it got in my face. Cian answered the door and smiled brightly at me.

"Come on. Nice to see you again, Lizzie," he said.

I gave him an affectionate smile and started up the steps behind him. "You too."

When I entered the apartment, it was quiet. There was no TV, no noisy boys, no nothing. "So, is Teagan here?" I asked, feeling uncomfortable. I didn't know if I wanted to see him now that I was actually there. The apartment felt familiar yet I was still a stranger. I couldn't help wondering what I had signed up for when I agreed to this outing. Evidently, I did want to see him since I was in his apartment, ready to spend a few hours with him, sober nonetheless.

The memory of his touch and his smile cooled my nerves a little. Then, I thought of Freddie's smile and that gave my

stomach a jolt, too. Maybe, subconsciously, I wanted to see
Freddie again, too. Fuck, my mind was playing games. You can't
want them both, Lizzie. Focus on Teagan. Freddie wasn't the one
who called.

"Yeah, he's getting dressed. He'll be out in a minute," he
replied and nodded his head to the couch. It was the same couch
Teagan and I spent hours talking, laughing, and kissing on and,
God help me, I quickly scattered to sit on the opposite couch.
Cian sat down next to me and pulled a sports magazine off the
circular table. I sat perched on the edge then realized I was too
nervous. Relax, Lizzie. Teagan is just a friend.

Teagan came out wearing a black shirt, black jeans and
Adidas sneakers. He came right up to my knees and looked down
at me, smiling so bright, I was momentarily stunned. His look
was so powerful and full of depth, there weren't any words. He
was such a bright light after the last two dismal days I had.

"Hey," I said, answering his smile.

"Hi, Lizzie," he said and sat down on the opposite couch.
The couch. *Our couch.* I looked at it slowly from side to side and
Teagan caught my look. He smirked, knowing that I was thinking
of being in his arms.

I pretended to play with the side loops on my Dickies as
he put both arms up around the top of the couch and looked at
me. Looking back at him with a half smile, I took in his looks.
His piercing blue eyes, dark, full eyebrows, slim lips, long jaw
and broad shoulders. Guys always looked better in your
memories but oh, those blue eyes. I could swim and get lost in
those eyes. I snapped myself out of my thoughts as I heard
Teagan say something to Cian about a bar and a game. I couldn't
care less what he was saying as long as he kept talking because

that sexy, fucking accent had me feeling a tightening in my panties. I needed to move. "So, you want to go? I'm double parked, and even though it's Sunday, I shouldn't risk getting a ticket."

"Sure," he replied as he started off the couch. He grabbed his light coat and winked at me as he pulled it on. I smiled shyly and immediately felt ridiculous. I had this guy's tongue in my mouth for hours. It was more than acceptable to wink at me.

We stood together and said our goodbyes to Cian, who didn't move his eyes from his magazine but offered up a goodbye as we headed out. Teagan opened both apartment doors for me and as we walked down the stairs to the car, he brushed his hand over the small of my back. I motioned to my car and we got inside. I turned to him.

"We can go to the Charles River and walk the path or we can head a little further out of town to a nature trail I know about," I said.

He shrugged and put his seat belt on. "It's up to you since you're from here. However, take me someplace where we can be alone," he replied. His accent was so thick it made me smile. I paused to stare at him, acting like I was trying to decide on our destination when in fact the butterflies came back in a rush. He was extremely fascinating and he was in my car. All mine and all alone. He smiled and motioned his hands to the road. "Get on. We don't want a ticket."

As Teagan looked through my CD case, we talked about music. He slid David Gray's CD in and turned the track to "This Year's Love." I glanced at him and told him it was one of my favorites. He gleamed back at me and said David Gray had played it the night before and mentioned how he swayed his head the whole time while he was singing. I laughed and as I went to put the gear into fifth. Teagan put his hand over mine and gently rubbed the top of my fingers with his. It sent shivers up my spine and I just couldn't look at him. Not once. The whole ride, I left my hand there and my face remained focused on the road. I softly sang along to David's deep voice, taking in the words and wondering if this was about Teagan and I. *"This year's love had better last. Heaven knows it's high time. I've been waiting on my own too long."*

Large oak trees lined the road and the leaves were in full bloom. It was so green and such a perfect day. I felt like my soul was being lifted with every second. I parked in the small area to the left of the nature trail and stared out the windshield to see if there were other people walking. I turned off the car and looked over to Teagan.

"I think we have the whole place to ourselves. Are you ready?" I asked with a big smile.

"Let's wait a few minutes in here. I want to talk to you," Teagan replied. I turned myself in the seat and waited for his next words.

"Well, I know you aren't as happy as you were when we were talking on the couch on Friday night," he said. "I want to know what happened to you since then."

I sat there looking at him, trying to understand how a complete stranger would notice a change in my demeanor. People in the past had told me I wear my emotions on my sleeve but those people were friends. I didn't discuss problems with complete strangers. Hell, when I had issues, I holed up in my room and didn't let anyone in. I always wanted people to see that nothing got to me. But for some reason, I was comfortable with

Teagan. His piercing blue eyes made me relax and I felt the truth being pulled out of my mouth.

"Darcy got into a car accident Friday night. She totaled her car, was arrested, and then taken to the hospital. I know that she isn't hurt…badly, but that's all I know because Conner, my brother, hates me right now. When I called to talk with her, her mother insinuated that I never call her house again. I'm a bad influence on everyone I come in contact with," I said that last part softly. It was like I was finally admitting to someone, and probably myself, that trouble followed me everywhere I went instead of deluding myself into thinking I followed trouble.

"Jesus Christ," he muttered while lowering his shaking head. He looked up to me with a serious look on his face that I couldn't decipher. Was he upset that I said I was a bad influence or just that Darcy was in deep shit?

"Listen," he said, "I don't know what to say other than I know for a fact that you tried very hard to stop her from driving that night. I know you demanded you wait to take her home after we bought you those drinks. You're blaming yourself and I can tell you're upset about that."

"Yes," I murmured, looking at the top hem of his black shirt and his straight chin.

He pulled his hand off the seat and tucked it under my chin to set his softened eyes on me. "You are not to blame. You are beautiful, inside and out. I have never seen a girl so determined to help out a friend. You were fierce. You are a good friend, no matter what anyone else says."

"Yeah, well, tell that to everyone that claims they love me," I said deferentially.

"I'm only in America for the summer. On August 17th, I head back to Ireland to finish my senior year at university. But, Lizzie, I like you a lot. I've thought about nothing but you over the last day and I was upset when I thought I might never see you again after Friday night. I like the way I feel when I'm around you. We didn't even talk on the ride here and it was more fun than I've had with a girl in a long time." He laughed. "I want to spend as much time with you as I can during this summer. However, I am leaving and I don't see myself coming back after I graduate. So, if you want, I would like us to be friends and get to know each other. Most girls want a relationship, and if I was an American, you would be my girlfriend. But, I'm not so that wouldn't be fair to either of us. Am I scaring you away?"

I was stunned. Nobody had ever been this forthright about a relationship, or in this case, lack thereof. What happened to one day at a time? I thought about the summer camps I used to go to and the boys I would kiss at the lake or in the dancehall. Shit, I never saw those guys again and they probably lived an hour away.

Teagan brushed his thumb across my cheek as he continued. "I understand if that… is not what you want. But I would like to hold you and hold your hand. I just want us to get to know each other in the next few months."

I thought about all the promises to call from one night stands that never came. I thought about the guys that I royally fucked over that actually wanted to have relationships with me and I just couldn't find a reason for a long term commitment. I thought about Chase telling me that he didn't see us ever getting married. I thought about this beautiful man in front of me, telling me that I would be, only could be his summer fling. An American girl. His American girl for a short period of time. For some reason, that flattered me. I felt special and yes, it would be the fun summer I was looking for. A nice memory for him of his time in America. He wouldn't or couldn't ever forget me. I would show him my feisty self, and besides, I always made a point to leave the guy with some sort of memory.

"Okay, just for fun," I said as I looked up to the clouds in the blue sky. I tried to process what I had just agreed to but decided it didn't matter. It was such a beautiful day and I wanted, no needed, to stay in the moment. I couldn't live in my past regrets and I didn't even want to think about the future. Teagan would be fun.

He smiled the widest smile I'd seen from him yet and opened his door to get out. When I met him at the back of the car, he took my hand with a firm grasp and we headed towards the trail. *So, the summer romance began.*

Teagan and I walked up the path towards the lookout point. The large green field stretched across to an amazing view of Massachusetts Bay Community College. We found a ledge of rocks to sit on and I motioned for him to join me as I plopped down. I pulled a Marlboro Red out of my pocket and lit it.

"Can I get one of those?" he asked.

I nodded and handed him a cigarette. After we stared at the green field in silence for a while, I pointed to the big brick building and said, "I'm starting school there in two weeks for summer courses. It's just two classes but I should start on my degree while I'm still young, right?" I smiled.

"Do you work?" he asked.

"No, not yet. I just got back into town. I have a few interviews this week for administrative stuff. I did some of that when I lived in Portland, so I'm sure I'll find something." I nodded with certainty. I really only had one interview with a small financial firm close to my house that paid minimum wage and looked like a data entry position. Boring data entry. It was a bit embarrassing, but Teagan didn't need to know that. I also didn't want to tell him.

I was taking the prerequisites for the actual accredited courses because I blew my SATs and all other gauging tests. Those important tests just weren't my thing. They measured how smart people were, and as far as I was concerned, I was average. Street smart was a whole different story, or so I thought.

I sat straight up and flicked my cigarette to the ground, half finished, and crossed my arms against my chest. I couldn't help feeling inadequate in that moment. Teagan would see there was nothing special in me eventually.

"Are you cold?" he asked in concern.

"Maybe a little. Oregon is milder than here. Even when it rains, there isn't a drop in the temperature. When it's blazing hot, then it drops 5 degrees, people notice in Boston. Plus, we're sitting in the shade," I replied, nudging him.

"Come here." He pulled himself back from the ledge, opened his arms to me then put me in between his legs. We sat quietly for a moment and a jolt of electricity went through my body when he nuzzled my neck, giving little tickles and licks. When he licked the back of my ear, I started laughing.

"Ticklish?" he asked with amusement as I looked at him.

"I guess so. I just didn't know I was ticklish there." I laughed.

"Hmmmm… Where else are you ticklish?" he asked playfully.

"I am NOT telling you that," I said urgently.

"Well, I guess I'll just have to find out," he said, amused.

"Maybe," I replied with a teasing voice.

He flicked his cigarette and twisted my body to face him. His warm lips kissed my red, cold nose then softly kissed my lips. We stayed like that, breathing each other's air in. He began to probe my mouth open with his lips until they parted, asking for more. When my tongue dipped onto his, his body shuddered and he immediately cupped my face. It wasn't messy. It was passionate and familiar from Friday night. It was demanding. We kissed as he held onto me so I didn't slide off the rock. Eventually, I realized that my hand was on the back of his neck, urging him for more.

I didn't really know Teagan, but in some way, he made me feel like I was the only girl in the entire world. I lost myself in his attention. I escaped the reality of who I really was and latched onto his lips like they would take me to a different self.

When I turned back around to face the view, I rested my hands over his and started to rub the cold from both of us.

In a quiet voice, he whispered into my neck, "Come stay the night with me again. Not on my couch. I want you in my bed." Well, that was certainly a bit forward. Talk about blunt conversations.

"You have a twin bed." I laughed, trying to hide my sudden unease by how fast he was moving.

"I room with Cian and he had to go to Chicago this morning, so the room is all mine for the next three days. Stay with me," he asked again.

"You start your new job tomorrow, right?" I asked, turning to look at him with a meaningful stare.

"We won't stay up too late," he said softly. "Come on. I'll make you pork chops and we can listen to music in my room."

"Sure, whatever," I agreed as I jumped off the proverbial ledge. If I had agreed to this summer thing, then I might as well start that night. It wasn't like I had anything else to do.

"Do you need clothes?" he asked.

I swayed my head back and forth slowly and said, "I haven't fully unpacked my car from my road trip so I have some stuff in the trunk."

"Trunk?" he asked.

"Yes, Mr. Gallagher. It's the place in the back of the car that you store things in," I stated with mock surprise. I felt like I was talking to a three-year-old.

"Ah. The boot." He laughed.

"Boot?" I exclaimed.

He jumped down, took my face in his hands, and gave me a quick kiss. After he turned to walk down the path, I kicked him sideways in the butt with my sneaker and said, "Now, that's a boot." He smiled at me, more seductively than he had before, and we held hands all the way down to my car.

Eight

Sleepover

Teagan and I didn't say much as we drove back to his
place. The silence was met with his soft touches and chaste looks.
He was warm and drew me in. His beautiful eyes made my
stomach do flip flops. While he played with the dials on the
radio, I could feel him glancing up at me like he wanted to ask
something. I couldn't get out of my own mind. Why was I willing
to spend the night with a guy that just said he couldn't give me a
future? The question just kept running over and over in my mind.
I finally looked over at him, asking him with my eyes what he
was trying to ask. All doubt of being with him was gone. He
wanted to be with me in that moment. That was it. I was a goner.

He squeezed my hand and asked, "Dinner?"

"Sure, what do you want?" I asked.

"There is an Irish pub around the corner from my place.
Do you want to get some food there? There's a hurling game on
TV too," he said with a grin.

"Okay. Just tell me where to turn."

Ten minutes later, we walked into Murphy's Pub and I
saw Kellan and Freddie sitting at a table with two other girls.
Okay, I guess our date was officially over. Teagan led me to their
table and everyone exchanged greetings. Teagan greeted the girls
with boisterous amusement. Freddie didn't acknowledge me at
all. That silent rejection made my stomach turn over. I guess he
didn't like me after all. After we ordered beers and burgers, the
game came on and everyone but me was immersed in the game.
Teagan tried to explain it as he was deep in trance with it. I didn't
get it. There was a stick called something sloiter and a method of

using your hands to make goals. I was thoroughly confused but no one seemed to notice. I was glad for that. It looked like field hockey and soccer at the same time. I ate my meal, sat back in my chair, and laughed when appropriate. Otherwise, I looked around the bar for something else to do.

I got up off my chair and quietly told Teagan I was going to check out the bar. He smiled at me and nodded. As I sat up at the bar stool, the bartender looked me over and mentioned something about liking the Counting Crows. I laughed and asked if he said that to all the girls with band names across their chests. He laughed back and started singing in my face to "*A Long December.*"

"Wow, I'm impressed," I exclaimed a bit loudly.

He gave me a wicked, cocky smile and handed me a new beer without me asking for one. Now there was the normal American guy, not leaving in three months. No hurling to obsess over. Free drinks and flirting was right there in front of me and yet, I was drawn to the unknown and unavailable for the long term. I realized in that moment I was not a long term girl nor had I ever been. I agreed to Teagan's company because of just that reason. There would be no dumping or bad endings. It would be fun with no strings attached.

Just then, two arms wrapped around my back and Teagan whispered in my ear, "What are you doing?" I swiveled around at him, unlocking his arms and glanced up to the TV. The game was still on. I nodded up to it.

"I'm watching the hurling." I smiled. Hmm… Teagan felt so good. Tingles went up my spine and this connection with him was a pleasurable leap from kissing and holding hands. It was possessive. It was thrilling.

"Sure, you are," Teagan bantered back to me. He nodded at my beer and took a drink from it, never taking his eyes off me. Looking into his eyes, I felt a surge of lust. I didn't care to know his favorite color or what he did in his spare time in Ireland or anything else. We didn't have to talk about Counting Crows or any more music. I wanted to stare into his eyes forever. I knew he felt it, too. He grabbed my hand and we rushed to his house without looking back.

Running into his room, his hands were all over my ass, my back and my neck. I giggled all the way down to his room and fell on one of the twin beds. He leaned over me and sighed. Ripping off his shirt, he said, "I fucked up." I gave him a quizzical look and he said, "We should have eaten our dinner in here." Aggressively, he pushed himself down on me and started kissing me with more intensity than before.

His hands moved up and down my arms and mine flew to his muscular shoulders. He groaned in my ear. My panties were instantly drenched at his wonderful sound. Oh, it was such a wonderful sound. I twisted him to his back and straddled him while his eyes never left mine. I ripped off my shirt and my black bra made Teagan step back. He sucked in a breath and said, "Beautiful." I smirked and laid my body on top of his.

After ten minutes of kissing and letting him explore underneath my bra, I rolled off him and almost onto the floor. He caught me and started laughing. "Where are you going?" he asked with total amusement.

"Nowhere. I mean, I wanted to ask if I got the bed right. Is this your bed?"

"Umm…actually no." He smiled. "This is Cian's. I guess we should move over to my bed, huh?"

"Yes. I don't really feel comfortable kissing you in another man's bed," I said with a laugh.

"You are so beautiful. Go get in my bed and get comfortable. I will go get us some beers," he said nervously, and headed for the kitchen.

I tossed myself face down on Teagan's bed. His pillow smelled clean. It smelled like Teagan and I was so excited for his touch again that I started squealing into the pillow. Suddenly, remembering I was only in my bra, I got really self conscious and started for my t-shirt. As Teagan came in, I had just pulled my hair out from underneath the back of my shirt.

"What are you doing?" Teagan asked, perplexed.

"Nothing. I mean, I just felt a little cold," I said, embarrassed.

We both fell silent after he gave me a bottled beer and sat down next to me on the edge of the bed. It seemed we were both in sync as we took swills from our beers. After a few minutes, I heard Freddie and Kellan come in the front door and music was turned on. I stood up and looked around the bare bedroom, taking interest in a large walk in closet, which was also extremely bare. From what I knew of Teagan, which was not much deeper than his major in college, he was a very simple guy. How had we spent so many hours kissing rather than talking? His bedroom didn't even tell me what his favorite book was.

"So," I said as I snapped my fingers together. "What do you want to do now?" He gave me a slight smile and put his arm around me, snuggling his mouth into my hair.

"I want you to take off your shirt again," he said slowly as he trailed his finger along my collarbone.

I squirmed away from him and laughed. "That tickles."

"Ah, maybe we should find out all of your tickle spots now that we are alone in a private place," he suggested with a big grin.

"No, no. I will take off my shirt! No tickling." I raised my hands up in surrender and he chuckled. He took the beer out of my hand and propped both bottles up against the wall. He turned me around to lay so we faced each other on his bed. We both started touching each other's faces and his hands followed the curve of my side. When he leaned in to kiss me, I forgot that I knew nothing about Teagan. I succumbed to the desire to be the center of his attention for as long as he wanted me. His kiss was slow and gentle but after several moments, the kiss grew deeper. He lifted the hem of my shirt and gave me a confident look as he stripped it off over my head. He didn't look at my chest. His eyes remained on mine. He grabbed my waist and murmured, "So soft." I felt the heat fall from my belly all the way to my toes. He chuckled. He must have felt the same spark.

"You're blushing," he said with a cocked eyebrow.

I buried my face in his shoulder and meekly said, "I'm sorry." He began to rub my back and I felt a sense of calm come over me. The past three days were automatically pushed out of my mind as I listened to the slow breath coming from his rising chest. I didn't think of Darcy and what she was going through. I didn't feel the broken distance from my brother. All I could think about was Teagan. He nipped at my shoulder while he rubbed his hands up and down my arms. Someone saw me. Someone wanted to hold me. Someone finally wanted to care. We started to pleasure each other through touches, murmurs, and intimate kisses everywhere.

Nine

Run Away

As I woke to the naked body beside me and the annoying alarm clock shrilling through the bare room, I groaned.

"Fuck," Teagan said under his breath. I immediately shot off the bed and slammed my hands down on the annoying clock, hoping to silence my swirling brain. How much did I drink last night? After recalling the night before, I shrugged off the feeling of disappointment. Teagan didn't have a condom so we couldn't have sex. That was good, I guess. Being safe was a good thing.

We discovered every inch of each other's body with our hands and mouths, sans a condom, until we were both too exhausted to continue. The living room party drew us of the bedroom. We joined the small crowd until we both stumbled to the bed, laughing at each other's missteps. He grabbed me and fully unclothed me. I was so tipsy, I didn't protest.

"I already don't want to go to work." He cleared his sleepy voice and looked over at me. "I want to sleep in the nude with you all summer long," he said as he stripped the sheets off of himself.

"That's good since it's ninety fucking degrees in this place with no air conditioning." I sighed. "Alas, Mr. Gallagher, you need to get going! It's your first day of work, Mr. Irishmen."

I snuggled up against his back as he tried to sit up and started rubbing his hands over his eyes. He looked over his shoulder at me and grinned.

"Go back to sleep," he whispered in a gentle Irish morning accent.

"Hmmm." I sighed.

He chuckled and I blocked out the rest of the bustling noise coming from Teagan and the other roommates by shoving the flat pillow over my head. The shower turned on and off but no one spoke. After a while, the front door closed and I drifted back to sleep.

At eleven, I heard the shrill of the alarm clock again. *What the fuck?* I stood to slam my hand on it again, only to realize it was coming from the kitchen. I scurried down the hall, pulling up my pants and without even thinking, I answered the ringing phone.

"Hello?" I said breathlessly.

"Lizzie! Good morning," Teagan said. His voice was deep and pleased.

"Hello, Teagan," I replied, feeling my stomach turning as I thought about what we did the night before.

"How are you? Are you getting on okay at my place?" he asked.

"Well, since I just woke up and I'm feeling kind of shitty from last night, I have yet to make that conclusion," I whispered, sighing. I sat on one of the bar stools and put my head on the kitchen bar.

"Are you going to make it?" he asked with a chuckle.

"Yup," I said. "I had a lot of fun last night. With you …and the guys, of course." His murmured agreement warmed my heart then it shuttered. This is the second time Teagan has called after a night of intimacy. He really does want to be in a pseudo relationship. Wow. I'd never been in this situation before and my heart tugged at my chest, picturing him picking up his desk phone at work to call me. My thoughts were cut off by a small creak of the door down the hall.

"Oh, I didn't realize one of the guys was still here," I said to Teagan.

"Oh, Freddie. He doesn't start working until Wednesday."

My heart started to flutter as I looked down at my Counting Crows shirt, reeking of beer, smoke, and sweat. "Okay, well, I'm heading out soon. Talk later?" I asked.

"What?" he asked surprised. "I mean, please stay. I should get out of here at four then a couple of lads and I are going to go to The Littlest Bar near the Commons. Come down and be with me. Plus, I stopped at the pharmacy this morning," he said in a suggestive manner.

"Well, I have those interviews and I have to start working on getting my books…" I trailed off, pausing on the part when he said he went to the pharmacy. My cheeks flamed up and oh God, for the first time, I felt suffocated and totally confused. I could have sex with a man when I was intoxicated but the mention of planning to have sex with Teagan made me a bit uncomfortable. I was speechless.

"Cat got your tongue?" He laughed. "Take down this number. The office gave me this fancy pager, so use it and let me know when you can come down tonight." He rattled off the numbers and I repeated them, looking down at the buttons on the phone, tracing over them with my fingers. Sometimes my photographic memory worked, and well, sometimes it didn't. We'd find out which.

We hung up, and when I raced back to Teagan's room to retrieve my things, I ran smack into Freddie. He pulled me up and smiled at me.

"Good morning," he said with a sincere smile.

"Morning," I mumbled. "I was just leaving. I have to head home."

"Ah, well I was going to make coffee. Do you want some before you head out?" he asked.

I felt myself suffocating even more. What the hell was going on with me? I liked being in Teagan's arms, but Freddie was something more. He wanted to have coffee with me now? He didn't even acknowledge me last night at the bar but he stared at me that night I first entered the house and didn't want to leave me alone with Teagan. I occasionally caught him watching me, unabashedly, the night before and he smiled directly into my eyes. Before I could smile back, he would snap his stare away.

"Lizzie?" he asked, concerned. "What are you thinking?"

"Umm...nothing. Coffee sounds great. Can I take a shower first? I'm disgusting."

He turned away to get a towel out of the closet and said under his breath, "Impossible."

Twenty minutes later, I walked out of Teagan's room with my hair wet and my bag over my shoulder. I was ready to leave. I felt like I was doing something wrong by being in Teagan's house without him.

"Hey, Freddie, I have to get going so I'm going to pass on the coffee," I said. I didn't want to go into any deep conversation with him. When he commented that it would be impossible for me to be disgusting, I knew it would happen. Freddie felt something for me. He was fighting it but it was there. I wouldn't encourage that. Eventually, he would see that I wanted to be friends and nothing else. Until then, there would be no Lizzie and Freddie in the same room alone. Stamped and approved. Thank you very much. He looked perplexed and nodded his head.

"So…see ya," I said, smiling.

"Bye, Lizzie. Hope we get to see you soon," he replied.

"Thanks. You too," I said meekly.

I couldn't help the sinking feeling that I was running away from Teagan and Freddie at the same time. Confusing! As I fiddled with the radio and put the car in gear, there was an overwhelming feeling that I wouldn't see them again in the same way as the first night we spent together. I knew it was impossible to already feel a pull toward them, but I did. I felt so comfortable partying with them and I was able to just be myself. Well, my drinking self. Ugh. I still wasn't feeling good from all the beers I had the night before.

Clearing my mind, I started to think about my new books at Mass Bay and the interview I had on Wednesday. I didn't know what I was more nervous about. I would most likely be in classes with eighteen-year-olds and that made me feel like a total loser.

On the other hand, the interview would go fine, but I didn't have the business casual attire. I thought about how inexperienced I was at appearing to have my shit together in the real world. I was sure that my previous experience with administrative work would impress them enough to do the data entry. Honestly, I didn't really want the job anyway but no one needed to know that. Pushing the thought back into my mind, I remembered Teagan's lips on my stomach and the inside of my thighs. I sighed. At least, I had experience in the Teagan department. Last night was so fun and yes, The Littlest Bar sounded like a good distraction.

Ten

Feud

As I headed into Wellesley, I saw Darcy sitting on a bench next to a smoothie bar. I immediately turned into a street spot, popped a quarter in the parking meter and headed towards her.

"Darcy!"

She looked up and smiled.

When I approached, we immediately exchanged looks that told each other how sorry we were. When we were within speaking distance, we spoke over each other about the fault and blame from the night of her accident. We held hands over the table as tears almost came to my eyes. Darcy's mother came out of the smoothie bar and stood still. When we both looked up, I tore my hand out of hers and she started to walk towards the table, sitting down, facing away from me. Darcy looked at her then glanced up at me with a sympathetic smile.

"Well, I'm glad you're well. Take care, Darcy," I said, defeated, and walked away. When I turned around, she had her hand up in a small wave. I knew that was the end of our friendship. Another one bites the dust. Just run away from the pain, Lizzie. There is no repairing the past. Did Darcy and Conner break up because of me? Fuck. I needed to talk to Conner.

I walked into the front door of my parents' sprawling white home that lay on the corner of a pristine neighborhood street of Wellesley. I dropped my bag next to the front door and headed to the kitchen for coffee. Mom and Dad were both at work, and if I knew his schedule right, Conner was attending his classes. When I turned into the kitchen, Conner was standing there, talking on the phone with a murmur. When he spotted me, he quickly said goodbye and hung up the phone.

"Lizzie," he stated in a hushed tone.

"Yes?" I asked. What fucking now, I thought, rolling my eyes while I grabbed the coffee pot.

"Lizzie, can we talk?"

I turned around and cocked an eyebrow at him while blowing the steam off my coffee.

"I'm worried about you. You came home only two weeks ago and while I imagine you are getting… umm… reacquainted with your old friends, you're never home. You didn't even call Mom or Dad last night. They were up half the night worrying and I had to pick up the mess, Lizzie. What's going on with you? The whole thing with Darcy was totally fucked up but now I know you did try to stop her but I'm still angry you drank," he stated with his hands in his pockets.

"Did you guys break up?" I asked. He sighed and shoved his fingers through his hair in frustration.

"No. Her mother doesn't really like you right now because she can't accept that Darcy would ever do something that stupid. Being that I'm your brother, I'm guilty by association and only get to talk to her on the phone for like thirty minutes a day." He shrugged.

I couldn't take it anymore. I knew it was my fault but for fuck's sake, I body slammed the girl. I begged her to wait just an hour or two so I could drink some coffee. If she hadn't been so quick to get out of there that night then I know events would have ended differently. But yes, it was my fault. I already felt it, knew it and lived with it every day

"You shouldn't have gotten pissed at her that night," I said blandly. "She wanted to leave because she thought you were going to break up with her if she didn't rush home."

He blanched. I cursed. I bowed my head and gave him a look that reminded him that I was aware of what I had done.

"Listen," I said. "I'm an adult and have been for over five years. I'm going to school and I'm getting a job this week. Whatever I do in my free time is my business. I am here temporarily. That's it. Shit, most of my friends are moving in with their boyfriends or freaking getting married! I am not trying to be a jerk and maybe I am, but I have tried to save face in any way possible with Darcy and her mother. I fucked up but I can't sit around alone and listen to other people tell me what I already fucking know!"

He threw up his hands. "THAT'S NOT THE FUCKING POINT, LIZZIE!"

"Yeah, I figured. Just lay off, Conner. Just forget about me. I'm not your problem," I replied in a flat tone and walked out of the kitchen. I didn't want to be yelled at after such a fucking wonderful night with Teagan. Jesus, every time I let loose and was myself, someone jumped in and reminded me how much of a piece of shit I was. Like they needed to tell me that to realize what I already knew. Just once, I wanted to be left alone. Just friggin once.

Conner followed me and continued to shout. I didn't know exactly what he said but it was a lot of cuss words about me being a fucking loser. I already knew that, asshole. I turned to stare at him while he continued to yell at me and nodded at him in the appropriate places until he was finished.

"I got it," I said with finality. I headed up the stairs and straight into the shower. I turned the water as cold as it could get and stood under it, trembling and crying. Conner always got me right where it hurt and it took a long time to mentally mute him. His words were swords and they hit my weakest points. Even though I always cried after Conner's outbursts, I'd never let him see me cry. The goose bumps that rose on my arms made me feel dead. I'm alive. I have a purpose. I'm alive. The thoughts just never seemed to sink in. The burning tears quickly merged with the cold water and I leaned my trembling lips into the shower until my tears left me. Cold showers were magic because they took the red out of my eyes.

After my shower, I headed to my room and found it partially open. Conner was sitting on my bed and looking at me as I walked in. "Look," he said, "I didn't want to scream at you. I'm not sorry for it but I shouldn't have yelled. You just don't hear anything these days. You aren't…well, you."

I pointed my finger at the door while holding my towel up around my chest and pressing my lips together. As Conner walked by, he dipped his dark red curly head and kissed me noisily on my cheek. When he left, I smiled. Conner was also very good at flipping the good brother switch on me. At times, those lectures made me cry more but today, I didn't have any more tears.

No matter how mad my brother got, he knew what it was like to have no direction in life. In the years before I moved out, I watched him drink himself into oblivion over and over. It wasn't until he got together with Darcy that he tamed his ways. I wondered if Darcy was his drink of choice now. If they broke up,

71

would he go back to his ways? I threw in "Under the bridge" by Red Hot Chili Peppers, turned it up to the highest volume level, and grabbed my guitar. I stared blankly out my window, and strummed my guitar to the song. The CD ended abruptly and I looked up to find Conner in the doorway.

"Are you even going to get dressed?" he asked, surprised as he pulled his finger from the pause button on the player.

"Yes, Conner, what the fuck is it now? Do you want a play by play on a day in the life of Lizzie O'Malley?" I asked.

"No, bitchy, there's a guy on the phone. Teagan?" He smirked with the phone pushed to his chest. "Do you want me to take a message?" I looked down at my guitar and strummed. Why is he calling me? Jesus, I'm so confused. He was starting to act a little creepy. I just talked to him, and while I was excited that he was obviously interested in me, I couldn't let myself be consumed by him. I paused and looked up to Conner for an answer. What would he think of this weird summer fling? I almost asked him but furrowed my brow and looked down.

"Yes. Tell him I'll call in a bit. Please get his number. I forgot it," I said. I couldn't remember the number. I guess maybe I didn't want to remember the number. I squinted at the ceiling, 617-555-1751? 1571? 7151? Fuck it.

I overheard Conner telling Teagan I was busy then it was quiet for a minute. I heard him laugh then he slid a piece of paper under my closed door. "He seems like a nice guy!" he yelled through the door. "I'm off to class. Leave the parents a note…better yet why don't you fucking call them?"

I rolled my eyes and headed to my closet to get dressed for the day.

Eleven

Little Shifts

Two hours later, the phone rang. I answered it. "Hello?"

"Lizzie, it's Teagan. Aren't you coming into the city tonight?" he asked.

"Um. I don't know. I have some things I need to get done," I said. I spent the past few hours thinking about this summer fling and strumming my guitar. It was uncharted territory and I was the master of uncharted territory. If I did everything he wanted, I would end up wasting my summer, never trying to reclaim my life back. I was confused about what Teagan really wanted and what I wanted. I came home to make something more of myself. Conner was right about getting my shit together, although I would never tell him that.

I didn't know what I was doing anymore. I wanted to be more than a party girl. I wanted to get on with my goals in life, although at that moment, I had no idea what those were. I sighed into the phone, feeling so confused and yet so defeated. I couldn't fail but something in me nagged that I already was failing. I wanted to feel excellent. I was sick of living inside my mind all the time. The strong desire to shove my head under the pillow and drown out the noise of the world no longer felt appealing to me.

"Don't be a poor sport. The guys and I are waiting for you right now. The Littlest Bar. Come now," he stated and then hung up.

An hour later, I drove into town and parked at Teagan's apartment, thankful for an open space. I scurried to Cleveland Circle and took the next available train to Downtown Crossing.

As I walked down the beautiful and old pebbled sidewalks, I no longer had apprehension about my tryst with Teagan and the summer to come. After Conner screamed at me, I decided to make some changes. I left a long note to my parents, with Teagan's number, assuring them of my safety. I felt a sense of relief. I didn't want to be at home. I didn't want to be under scrutiny. I didn't want people that I loved questioning my every move. That's why I left for Oregon in the first place. But now, I was given the opportunity to do it in the city I adored and with people I hardly knew. Frankly, Wellesley and every other place fell away and I was on my own again. I smiled outwardly because I felt free. I was independent and there was no one to answer to.

The intense feelings for Teagan grew stronger as I stepped into The Littlest Bar. I was taken aback. Teagan wasn't kidding when he said it was little. It doubled in size to Teagan's walk in closet and had at least eighty people crammed into it. Gaelic music pounded through a sound system, drowning out the multiple shouts for more beers and loud conversation. There were no televisions and no seats. That place was the equivalent of a cluster fuck. Holy hell.

I like to pride myself in enjoying a good party but this cramped space was overwhelming and I felt an anxiety attack coming on. I lifted my hand to my heart and realized I was being pushed in by people trying to get to the small bar. I stood on my tiptoes, trying to find at least one familiar face. When Teagan looked up to the door in anticipation, his eyes found mine and he gave me the downright sexiest smile ever. I stood still while a shutter passed down into my stomach. He plowed his way through the crowd and handed me a bottled beer. Because it was so loud in the bar, we just looked at each other. The nonverbal conversation was once again intact. We spoke so many words with just our eyes and expressions that I couldn't wrap my head around them. In that moment, I believed in fate and he was mine. People shoved me from all sides and he noticed. He quickly drew me in front of him, guarding me from the people assaulting me. He threw his head down and yelled, "I'm glad you made it." I smiled up to him and nodded. His whole demeanor changed in that bar. His first glance at me, when we saw each other, although intense and happy, became something else. I was in his home. He was at peace in this chaos, holding onto my waist. I squeezed his hand that was on my waist and took a long draw of my beer.

"Have I told you that you're so sexy when you drink like that?" he asked. "And, Jesus, you look amazing. I want to strip you down and lick you everywhere."

Although I heard him, I couldn't speak. The last thing I ever expected from a guy was to say my drinking was sexy, and the way my panties just got wet from his words was crazy. I was stunned. I couldn't look at him. I couldn't move. Again, my heart twisted and I felt like this complete stranger knew exactly who I was and accepted me unconditionally. Had I ever craved that kind of praise? Had I ever felt so turned on and so in lust by someone I hardly knew? I shook my head from the thoughts and turned to focus on the ever growing crowd.

Teagan, never loosening his grip on my waist, started laughing and shouting at people around him. I noticed I was only one of five girls in the packed space and quickly understood his wrap on me. He was letting people know I was his. Men were looking at me and Freddie, at the bar, glanced in my direction several times. Once our eyes met, I smiled and he nodded slowly. He glanced down at Teagan's hands around my waist then went back to talking to the bartender, an older, gray-haired Irishman behind the bar. Thick accents enveloped me as I felt myself being swept away in this foreign place only steps away from the familiar city I knew so well. Except tonight, I didn't know my surroundings at all. For once in a long time, I honestly didn't give a shit.

"Teagan? I want a shot," I yelled.

He smiled down at me and we made our way to the bar where we proceeded to down multiple shots of whiskey.

Hours later, Teagan and I left The Littlest Bar and headed to the T. Initially, I objected because I was having a great time but in no uncertain terms, Teagan whispered that the night was not over. As we stumbled to the T, Teagan put his arms underneath me to keep me straight as we walked over the cobblestone street to the Boston Common station. His hold never faltered even as we passed the turnstile and rushed to get on the next train. Although there were open seats, we held onto the bars as we looked into each other's eyes. He dipped his head into my hair and started kissing the back of my neck. Then his lips were on mine and as I stood there, swaying side to side with the train, his tongue plunged into my mouth, and we devoured each other during the ten stops to Cleveland Circle station. We didn't even notice we got there until the automatic woman's voice came on and announced the stop. Immediately, we tore apart and ran to the doors just before they started to close.

Back in the apartment, we skipped the pleasantries to his roommates and immediately headed to his bedroom. He took off his tie and dipped back on his bed, face up. When I started to him, he put his hands up, halting me.

His stormy eyes looked up to me and quietly, he said, "Lizzie, will you please strip for me? I want you so bad. For days, I've dreamt and thought of you doing this for me."

I smiled and lifted my shirt. I slowly removed my bra and, when I had removed my pants, I stood there with my underwear still in place.

"You have to finish the rest," I said.

He crooked his finger and we immediately started on each other's mouths, just as we had on the train. His fingers led up and down my back and he swore.

"I want you, Teagan," I whispered over his lips.

He immediately twisted me off him and took control. He held his body over mine and stared me up and down before pulling a condom from underneath his pillow.

As I smiled up to his determined face, he looked impatient but sheepish. "I want to do this so bad. I won't be good the first time. I've wanted you since the very first night, so I have to apologize before we do this," Teagan said.

I put my hand on the side of his face and gave him a quick nod of approval. Within minutes, he had kissed every part of my body, like he had promised at the bar, and slowly slipped himself into me. Both of us gasped when he was completely inside of me then he looked down into my eyes to make sure I was okay. I smiled and he rolled himself out of me. I closed my eyes and he rocked back into me a bit more aggressively as he reminded me how sexy I was and how nothing had ever felt so wonderful in his life. I said nothing. I just felt the rocking and moaning and the swirling air around me that took me to another exhilarating place.

After we reached our climaxes, we were both panting so hard we couldn't even speak. We lay there in the dark and cuddled up to each other. As we got our breath back, he whispered to me, "Lizzie."

77

"Yes?" I asked.

"I want this every night. I want this every night with you until I have to go back home. I know you have other obligations, but I have a key for you and I want you here every night, with me, in my arms," Teagan said in his thick Irish accent with a shining delight in his eyes.

"Umm…okay, Teagan, but where is Cian going to be?" I asked. Of course, I would sleep wherever Teagan wanted me to. I let go of Conner and the expectations from my family and stepped into the Ireland of Boston. Teagan was fun and he paid for all our drinks and the sex was amazing. In just a few days, we knew each other's bodies like old lovers. He could be sensual one moment and then he became a desperate animal. I didn't want anything other than that. No strings attached, pseudo relationships might look pretty damn good on me. The summer would be all about being. Living in the moment and enjoying the ride.

"Ah, Cian. Yes, well, we can make a bed up in the closet," Teagan laughed.

I dropped my head on my elbow as I shook my head at him and smiled.

"Teagan, I enjoy you. I enjoy being in your world. My world has been, well, turned upside down and everyone takes me so seriously. But when I'm with you, that all falls away and I feel safe. I feel like a whole different person. Maybe you bring out the real person in me because I haven't laughed more with another guy in my life. I haven't been held like this by anyone. You're temporary, I know, but I'm okay with that. It's just fun, and I'll go on this ride with you until it stops," I said with excitement.

"Do I satisfy you, Lizzie? In the bed, I mean?" Teagan asked.

I laughed. "There are a lot of things we can experiment with, Teagan. I have no problem with that department. You and I have chemistry. Right from the beginning, I felt a connection to you. The sex is, well, just a bonus. I love being in your arms, you being inside me. Somehow, in some strange way, it just completes our bond. Does that make sense?"

Teagan nodded, smiled at me, and brushed his hand along my face. I leaned back into him, and as our breaths started to even, all I thought about was the beating of my heart and how nothing could feel more perfect than that moment.

Twelve

Shots

Two weeks later, I had literally moved in with Teagan, Cian, Freddie, Kellan and Aidan. Most of my clothes were now in the walk-in closet and the textbook I was attempting to read lay beside Teagan's bed. The guys seemed happy to have me around because I was a female, after all. I washed up after meals and cleaned up after parties. I thought it was a far better way to pay rent than with money. Besides, when I tried to give Teagan rent money, he was insulted so I didn't push too hard. Apart from showing off every morning with eggs and coffee, I always had the beers stocked and ready for them when they came home.

The weekends were my favorite times. Every Saturday, we headed to the park near their apartment, where I was engrossed in their hurling practices. I still didn't understand how the game was played, but hell, there were a lot of sexy, sweaty guys, whose shirts may or may not come off, depending on the temperature. From behind my sunglasses, I not only appreciated my Irish boy toy, but the rest of the beautiful scenery. The scrimmages were intensified by their determination, choice words in their thick accents, and the occasional mud that spread across their sexy chests. Most times, I sat and worked on homework, and since I had blown off the interview that Wednesday due to the worst hangover ever, I decided my lot in the present time was to be their American token female. Most people would label me their bitch, too, but I didn't really mind. The fun outweighed the chores by far.

There were hardly ever other women at the apartment but when they did come over, the guys included me as a roommate, always pointing out that I was Teagan's girl. Teagan never protested that label and his eyes never strayed far from me. Even when we were across the room from each other, we spoke with our eyes. We could hold hour long conversations about what we wanted to do to each other's bodies that night. His hands, his lips, and his body became like my second skin and it was amazing. The only problem with the living situation is that I was discomforted by Freddie. He was weird around me. He and I never got past hello and goodbye. I often wondered if I was especially intruding on his space. When I mentioned my concerns to Teagan, he immediately discounted my thoughts. He said Freddie was a private guy and I shouldn't worry so much. The discomfort level shifted one Saturday when Freddie got hurt in the shin at a practice and was sent to the sidelines.

Instead of sitting with his team, he came over to the blanket I brought out and sat next to me without saying a word. Immediately, tension coursed over me. I couldn't figure out what to do. Part of me wanted to bolt to the apartment. Part of me wondered if he came to my blanket for a reason. I decided to wait it out, trying to read my book. Finally, I was going to jump out of my skin if one of us didn't say something.

"Hey, Freddie," I said with a concerned look. "Feeling okay?"

"Ah, yeah. No problems. My head wasn't really in the game today. I probably drank a little too much last night." He smiled.

"I'm there with you. I have a killer hangover. This morning, I was forced to have a little hair of the dog that bit me. Except, I'm not sure what type of dog bit me, so I had to sample quite a few drinks this morning to get it just right." I laughed.

"So what are you up to tonight? I heard that Teagan is going out." he asked.

"Huh? Aren't we all going out?" I asked.

"Yeah, well, no. Teagan has some business thing tonight. He didn't tell you about it?" he asked with a slight grin on his face.

"No," I said with a frown. "I guess I'll just head back to my house for a quiet night." I shrugged my shoulders and acted like I didn't care. But, fuck, I really did care. Teagan and I were inseparable. Besides, Teagan always told me what was planned for us every evening. Maybe he had told me and it slipped my mind.

"Jesus, the guys and I can't get him to stop talking about it. I guess it has something to do with him getting a job in Ireland when he gets back home. I'm really surprised he didn't say anything," he said before chugging an orange Gatorade.

"Hmmm," I murmured nonchalantly, looking back down at the paperback of Pride and Prejudice. I mentally ignored the image of Teagan having a job anywhere but Boston and his upcoming return to Ireland. The looming date of his departure started to bring dread into my heart. Maybe I'm getting in way too deep with Teagan if I already hurt that much when I thought of his leaving. There was no sense in getting upset with something I couldn't control.

"Do you want to go out with me and a few of my other friends in town? Today is actually my birthday," Freddie said.

"Freddie! Your birthday? Why didn't you tell me?" I asked. I shouldn't have been surprised because he actually hadn't spoken more than two words to me since the first night we met. I immediately threw down my book, wrapped my arms around him, and gave him a smacking kiss to his face. He flinched.

"It isn't a big deal, but it would be fun if you came along," he said and shrugged.

"That would be fabulous, but first, I have to go out and buy something special for your big day!" I said as I pushed away from him and started to collect my things. Dad's allowance was still going in weekly so I knew I had enough for a fantastic present.

"Lizzie! It really isn't that way. Please don't make it a big deal. It is just a few friends. No need to go out and get presents," he protested.

"Too bad, Freddie," I said as I thumbed my nose at him. Freddie got up and started to chase after me as I ran down the street, laughing. After slowing down, I side kicked him on the ass and he wrapped his sweaty arm around my shoulder as we walked the five blocks back down to the guy's apartment. When we made it to the steps, I watched him walk inside and smiled.

"What time do I need to be back for the night?" I asked as I looked at my watch.

"We'll be ready to leave at six. Dinner first, then the club."

"Okay! I'm off to find my second most favorite Irishmen the best American birthday gift in the history of mankind," I said as I headed off to my car.

"Lizzie," he called after me.

"Yes?" I asked.

"What should we tell Teagan? I mean, we just left him without a word. You didn't even say goodbye," he said.

I shrugged. I didn't really care about Teagan at that moment. I felt offended by him. Why didn't he ask me to go to dinner? Was he just going to leave me behind?

I waved it off and said, "Oh, he's fine. If he has that dinner thing tonight, I'm sure he'll be really happy about me hanging out with you guys. No biggie. Just tell him I needed to go get a gift, okay?" I asked.

"Umm…yeah sure," he said hesitantly.

Thirteen

Presents

I was normally very good at picking out presents for friends. Always very in tune with other people's desires, I tried to find gifts that were solely for the person's enjoyment. However, shopping for an Irishmen, especially one that I wasn't intimate with, turned out to be a little difficult. Knowing that Conner was away on a tour with The O'Malley Band and my parents were up in Maine on Peak's Island for the weekend, I set out to my house in Wellesley to quickly compose a funny birthday jingle on my guitar.

While I ate a California sandwich, I silently thanked my parents for always keeping the house stocked with good food, because damned if I wasn't sick of bar food and take out. As I sat at the table, writing and laughing to myself, I was startled by the loud ringing of the telephone. Normally it wasn't that loud, but for some reason, it seemed to shrill. Before I answered, I lowered the volume of the ringer.

"O'Malley residence," I said quickly.

"Lizzie! You're home? I didn't know what happened to you!" Teagan said, franticly.

"Teagan? Aren't you supposed to still be playing?"

"Well, yes, I was. But during the break, I noticed you were gone and when I asked around, no one had seen you leave. Why are you at your parents?"

"Oh, so you didn't go back to your place yet?" I asked while taking the phone from my ear to double check the caller ID. Yes, he was home.

"Yes, I'm here but you aren't," he replied stiffly.

"Didn't Freddie tell you I went off to go shopping?" I asked, confused.

"No. Freddie isn't at hurling or here. What's going on, Lizzie?" he asked impatiently. "I thought we were going to spend the rest of the afternoon together."

"Well... I ran into Freddie on the sidelines at the hurling game and he told me today is his birthday." I said with a cheer. "So, after he explained you had plans tonight with your work or coworkers or whatever, he asked me to join him for his birthday dinner with some of his other friends in town. I came home to grab my guitar and I'm writing a funny jingle for him. Hey, what do you think I should buy him? I only want to spend about fifty bucks but I have absolutely no clue what he is into."

Teagan sighed heavily. What the fuck? Why was he sighing at me? The phone went silent and I brought the phone back from my ear to see if we were still on the line. We were.

"Teagan? What's up?" I asked, frustrated with his silence.

"Lizzie, I told you about the dinner last weekend. Remember? I only have to go for two hours then I was planning on spending the night with you alone. Why are you going to hang out with Freddie?" he asked.

"I dunno. I just thought it would be fun. I didn't realize you wanted to see me after the dinner. In fact, you never told me about the dinner at all or I would have called up one of my girlfriends to hang out with. Was I drunk when you told me about it? No one is home here and I'm actually eating something nutritious for the first time in weeks," I said, laughing.

Teagan didn't laugh back. He was silent. I could literally feel him brooding through the receiver. Moments passed and I couldn't take it anymore.

"So," I said, "why don't you go to your dinner then come join us at Freddie's party? I don't think anyone would mind."

"I wasn't invited. None of us were, Lizzie. It's a little weird that he invited you out of all of us," he said.

"Oh, well, maybe he felt bad for me or something," I said, popping a fresh green grape in my mouth.

"So when am I going to see you?" he asked.

"I'm just about finished up here and it's what, two thirty? So I should be there about four," I said. He exhaled loudly and murmured something under his breath that I couldn't comprehend. Were we having our first argument? This shouldn't be a big deal. Teagan wasn't my keeper and, Jesus, he had plans anyway. I mentally told him to calm the fuck down.

"Teagan, I'm not doing anything on purpose. I came home to grab the guitar then I'm heading to get Freddie a present, and then I'll be there," I said.

"Okay. I have to leave by four thirty to get downtown on time, so hopefully I'll see you before I leave."

"Yes. I'll put a move on it. Hey, don't worry about it. We have tomorrow to hang out and I'll be in your bed tonight, making sweet sexy noises in your ears," I said with a grin.

He laughed, seeming to relax a little bit, and told me I better be prepared for our wicked night ahead.

Half an hour later, I was standing in Ben's Liquor Store in Waltham, ringing up the biggest bottle of Crown Royal they had. I would make it to that apartment before Teagan headed out so he wouldn't be worried during his work dinner.

When I arrived at the apartment at three forty-five, I headed towards Teagan's room to put my guitar and present for Freddie in the walk in closet. Hell, we weren't going to be demonstrative. Teagan was standing in the closet, looking perplexed while he held out two ties. When he looked up at me, he smiled wide. God, I would never get enough of that smile. He was simply perfect for me.

"Hey there." He held up the two ties, silently asking for my opinion, and I pointed at the blue pin striped one.

"It goes with those beautiful Irish eyes," I said.

He came up close to me, wrapping his arms around my waist. I leaned my forehead on his. I breathed him in and felt that sense of comfort once again. I would never get enough of his touch either.

"Are you okay?" I asked.

"Yes. I'm just a little nervous about this dinner, and I didn't know Freddie was going to invite you out. I just talked to him and it's fine. You'll have a good time with him and his friends. They're good people," he said stiffly.

We kissed sweetly and he patted my butt as I started out of the closet to get ready. I hadn't had time to get changed at my house. I closed Teagan's door and locked it. When he came out and saw me topless, he froze.

I laughed at him while I threw on my strapless bra and new blue satin tank. Then I shimmied out of my jeans and threw on a khaki skirt with buttons up the front. When I bent over to put my heeled sandals on, Teagan was right behind me.

"Jesus. You're getting really dressed up for the party. You're so sexy," he said while kissing my neck.

"Well, you don't look so bad yourself." I smiled. We sat on the bed and talked about how to meet up later and he assured me that he'd see me in the next few hours. I hugged him, inhaling him in. God, couldn't we just skip the night and spend it in the sleep pad? Ugh, the thoughts I had from just his scent. I squeezed his ass. He jumped then turned into me, sliding his hands up my thighs.

"Oh no," I said. "We are already dressed."

"Dressed? You look naked." He laughed while nibbling at my ear. He coaxed me into an intense make out session, like we wouldn't see each other for weeks.

Teagan kissed me sweetly and I started out of his bedroom, guitar in hand to go to the living room to play until it was time to go.

Freddie walked in and I went still. He was dazzling. No, he was downright delectable. He wore a black polo shirt that looked brand new and jeans that hugged his long toned legs. His inky black hair was styled in some gel and his eyes were brilliant as he looked at me. He gave me a knowing look like he understood that I was happily drinking him in.

"Hey," I said, sounding a bit squeaky.

"Hey. What are you playing? I didn't know you're a musician," he said with his thick Irish accent.

I laughed. "I'm not really. My brother, Conner, is in a band and I kind of got hooked on his music. He taught me some chords and I play around. I don't know much more than a little Pink Floyd, and don't laugh, Happy Birthday."

He smiled me and nodded, as if to tell me to go on.

"Okay, see if you can name this tune. You really have to listen because I'm not that good," I said hesitantly.

I propped up the guitar over my bare thigh, since my khaki skirt was kind of hitched up a little too high, and started to strum.

"Ah, Tom Petty. American Girl," he said with a wicked smile.

"Yes, I am. I mean, I'm an American girl. Not Tom Petty," I looked at him pointedly.

"No, Lizzie, you're not. You sound pretty good," he said as he sat down next to me. He took the guitar out of my hands and looked down at my leg before quickly darting his eyes away from me. As he started to pluck strings like he knew how to play, which he obviously didn't, I laughed and stood up.

"Hey, where are you going? I'm not that bad, am I?" he asked.

"No. Not at all. You're a natural," I said with a wry smile. "I'm going to get your birthday present. We might as well get it out of the way now," I said.

A few minutes later, I came out with the purple and blue Crown Royal box and handed him a card. His eyes looked up to the box then he gaped at me. Something wild was in his eyes. I shrugged it off like it wasn't a big deal.

"We have to take a few shots of this then you can have the real present. I need some liquid courage," I said.

"Lizzie," he said, astounded. "This must have cost you a fortune."

"Nah," I said, waving my hand. "Plus, you're going to share so it's really a present for the both of us."

He went into the kitchen and grabbed some shot glasses. When I looked around the apartment, I scanned in on Freddie and asked, "Where are the rest of the guys?"

"There were some college girls they wanted to party with tonight," he said with a laugh.

I giggled at the thought of Kellan pulling off his pants and standing on tables. Those college girls were in for a show from the wild Irish boy. I wondered if any of the girls would run for their lives.

Freddie sat down next to me and poured us both shots. I raised my glass to his and said, "To getting older!" He laughed and we downed them. I darted off the couch, the burn almost scorching my throat to shreds, and he darted the other way, gasping and cursing.

"Well, maybe I should have gotten something smoother," I said with a scowl.

Freddie looked at me as my face flushed from the shot and said, "No, this is perfect. This is the best birthday present I've ever received."

I laughed at him while he poured our next shots. We linked our forearms around each other and took the shot. Not too bad the second time around. I nodded my head with an appreciative face and picked up the guitar that was leaning up against the couch.

While he poured the next two shots, I played songs for him to guess then I started singing along. Eventually, Freddie got into it too and we sang until our voices were strained. It was official. We were on our way to drunk.

Before our next shot, Teagan walked out and came straight to me. With his eyes glued to mine, he took the glass out of my hand and threw it back, barely flinching at the burn. He leaned forward and gave me a deep kiss, filling my mouth with the taste of his shot.

"I'll be back soon." Teagan said.

I nodded, unable to speak.

He walked out the door without looking at Freddie once.

"Hey," I said as I cleared my throat. I turned to Freddie and slapped him on the chest. He mocked hurt and I gave him a look that clearly said, "Bullshit." He laughed at me then put his hand on my thigh. I looked down to it and then up to him. He looked happy, probably the happiest I'd ever seen him. But suddenly, I was uncomfortable with his subtle touch.

"When do we leave for your birthday dinner?" I asked.

He glanced down at his watch and his eyes widened. "Oh shit, we were supposed to be at Downtown Crossing ten minutes ago," he exclaimed, jumping off the couch.

I ran down the hall and stashed the bottle of Crown and my guitar in the walk in then ran out with my purse slung over my head. I was definitely wobbling already. Okay, Lizzie, sober up. There's a whole night ahead of us. Shit, getting drunk early was not the best recipe for a night out on the town.

Luckily, we hit the next green line train downtown quickly, and as we sat, we laughed and hummed all the songs we had just been playing. Freddie was so easy to talk to. He was like hanging out with Conner back when we were shitfaced together and had no cares in the world. People stared at us but we didn't care. When we got off at the downtown station, he grabbed my hand and headed over to two guys waiting by a cart outside of a CVS pharmacy.

Freddie quickly introduced us then apologized about our tardiness. I couldn't remember their names if I tried, however, both eyed me and Freddie with knowing looks. Obviously, they could see we were drunk. They were amused more than anything. Our arms were linked and we kept the secret of the Crown Royal to ourselves. His touch was nice. It was friendly and his cologne was almost as intoxicating as the whiskey. I thought about Teagan and what he was doing at that moment. Was he thinking about me? I hoped to see him soon. In the meantime, it was Freddie's birthday and we were having a blast.

Joe's Crab Shack was crazy with people. Waitresses with tight shirts and big boobs carried our steaks, shrimp, and burgers. The four of us grabbed a booth seat after waiting for what seemed like forever and immediately ordered drinks and appetizers. Freddie and I sat on one side and the two other guys, names still not remembered, sat on the other side. They hardly gave much notice to us as they stared at the four girls sitting opposite us. Freddie talked about his job for a while, and after I started to mentally yawn, I excused myself to powder my nose.

Instead of heading to the restrooms, I went straight to the waitress station, swaying the whole way and apologizing to everyone that I bumped into. I asked if they could deliver a piece of cake for the special birthday boy. They said they would send one over after we finished our dinner. When I got back to the table, the guys that we were with were standing at the girls' table, and Freddie was sitting there, smiling at me with his cheek on his hand.

"Lizzie! Let's dance!" he exclaimed.

I looked around the restaurant then looked back at him, perplexed. Dance? Dance where? I shrugged my shoulders and peeked up to him.

"It's the next level down," he said. "They started the music at eight. I can hear it already."

I stopped to listen. It had gotten quite noisy in the restaurant. I held out my hand to Freddie and smiled at him. As we headed down the ramp to the next level, I swear I heard my name from behind my back. When I looked around, no one was there. Freddie was pulling me along so hard that I was literally tripping over my feet.

We hit the dance floor with excitement. Techno pop radiated over the vinyl floor and we started to dance with each other. We bumped and grinded with each other. It was so fun and Freddie was a great dancer. When one song went into another, he leaned over to my ear and I moved in to hear him.

"You should have picked me that night at Mary Ann's, Lizzie," he said. His face was so intense. He wasn't yelling at me, but his voice was fierce.

I stopped dancing and just stood there in total shock, staring at him. After a long pause, I mouthed, "What?" to him and he just shook his head while taking me back into his grasp to dance to the groove of the music. I felt warm hands come around my side and pull me back. My vision was a little blurry from all those shots and the dancing. I twirled around and found Teagan standing there, looking stern and pissed off.

"What the fuck are you doing?" he asked.

I stepped back from Teagan and at the same time, Freddie brushed past me towards the table. I looked over Teagan's shoulder to see that Freddie was pissed, too. What the hell? In my drunken state, I could only comprehend two things. Number one, Freddie may have just told me that he thought of me as more than a friend, and number two, Teagan was turning into an obsessive, jealous boyfriend. I stood there feeling perplexed. Teagan could see the alarm on my face, too. His face softened and he took my hand. He led me back to the table where our full appetizers, dinner, and Freddie's cake were sitting untouched. No one was at the table. I turned all the way around and couldn't see any of the guys I had actually come there with. Whatever. This was awkward. I sat down on the bench and Teagan squeezed in tighter and put one arm on the back of the booth and one on the table, blocking me from not only getting out but any visuals on where Freddie had gone to.

"Look at me, Lizzie," Teagan ordered.

"Teagan, you're kind of scaring me. Why are you being so mean? I was dancing with Freddie. I was celebrating his birthday—"

Teagan cut me off. "He was about to kiss you, Lizzie. What the mother loving hell is Freddie doing trying to kiss you?" he asked firmly.

I blanched. I was at a loss for words. My mind ran through the last twenty minutes of events. I didn't see Freddie try to kiss me, and I certainly wasn't going to kiss him back. That was ridiculous. I examined the hard lines of Teagan's beautiful face. Where was my sweet and fun loving Teagan, and who the hell was this guy in front of me? Why was he taking my going out with Freddie so badly? Did he know that Freddie had a thing for me before tonight? A million thoughts of what to say back to Teagan ran through my head. Like, "please fuck off" or "honey, you are being silly" or "Teagan, get a grip..." None of those answers seemed adequate because I was dancing with Freddie really close and I had essentially blown off Teagan to be with Freddie. My whole day was consumed with it being Freddie's birthday and, shit, I had forgotten to sing his funny jingle to him. Good God. Was I being a shitty American summer fling? For fuck's sake, no one knows the rules about these sorts of things. Teagan and I hung out every day. Yes, we basically had sex every night and it was always good. It was fun and intense, but this dark, jealous side wasn't something I ever anticipated from him.

"Lizzie, will you please leave with me now? We need to talk," Teagan said.

"Teag, what's going on up there?" I said as I pointed to his head. "I slept in your bed last night and have for the last three weeks. You and I are inseparable when you aren't at work and when I'm not at school. I know I wasn't with you today, but Freddie and I are just friends. We have been friends from the beginning, and while I might have flirted and danced with him, I was not a conniving slut. I would never kiss Freddie. We were just having a good time. We drank a lot of Crown Royal and we were trashed before we even got here. So, I'm sorry if you think you saw something that wasn't actually happening, but nothing was happening. It's in your head. You and I have this arrangement for the summer, and I'm not interested in pursuing anyone else sexually," I said decisively.

Teagan sighed and looked at me with resignation.

"I don't want to leave. I'm having a really good time. I think it would be rude to Freddie if I just left. I didn't say a word to him and I haven't paid for my part of the meal. Shit, I even ordered him this piece of cake!" I said, mustering up some enthusiasm.

Teagan released his intense gaze on me, sat back, and rested his head on the back of the booth. He picked up one of the full glasses of beer on the table and drank it down. After sitting there for a minute, he looked over at me and smiled. He turned his gaze to my legs, because, of course, my skirt was once again hiked up. Anyone looking hard enough would be able to see my cotton white undies. God, I love cotton white undies on summer nights. Teagan slid his warm hand over my knee and up to the hem of my skirt. I looked at him with mock surprise and wrapped my arms around his neck. After giving him a big fat smooch on the lips, I looked up to see Freddie across the table from me, eating the chocolate cake even though the unlit candle remained in the middle of it and no one had sung Happy Birthday. I didn't even realize he had come back to the booth. None of us touched our dinners. It was uncomfortable. When Freddie looked up at me, his eyes were blazing. Passion? No. Anger? No. It was something else. His gaze stung me and I gave him a slight smile. He was trying to say something to me telepathically about Teagan as his eyes flicked over to Teagan. Maybe he was upset that Teagan had showed up at all. Did I mention to Freddie that Teagan might show up?

Freddie and I were having such a great time and now I felt the heavy weight of a man's jealousy on my shoulders. This was clearly not a summer moment of fun. Freddie pursed his lips together and looked back down at the cake. I sat there looking between Teagan and Freddie, wondering what the hell I was supposed to do next. I decided to look anywhere but at the two guys in the booth. Everyone around us was having a great time and I was being sucked into a crappy evening.

After several minutes, the waitress came by and Teagan threw his credit card on the table to pay for the meal, even though he wasn't invited and no one had actually eaten. Well, shit. I grabbed the waitresses' attention and order three shots and handed her my card. Teagan waved my card away and told the waitress to put it on the rest of the bill. The tension between Teagan and Freddie was palpable and I hated it.

The waitress came back with the three shots. I needed to lighten the mood and bring back some of the summer sparkle into the night. I took my shot and placed the other two in front of Teagan and Freddie.

"Okay guys, bottoms up. Cheers to birthdays and Irishmen!" I saluted.

They both gave me tight smiles and took down their shots. Freddie slammed his glass down on the table and I jumped.

Teagan eyed him with curiosity. I winced at their obvious testosterone battle. Ugh. This was a disaster.

Teagan leaned over and whispered with a plead in his tone, "Lizzie, if we can't go home, will you at least come out to the sidewalk and talk to me for a few minutes?"

I rolled my eyes towards the wall and nodded my head.

"Freddie, we'll be right back. Don't go anywhere. You and I have another half of Crown Royal to drink tonight," I said with a wry smile.

Freddie smiled and nodded up to me as I started out of the booth. He leaned back and eyed Teagan's hold on my hand.

When we made it to the outside sidewalk, I eyed Teagan, trying to gauge his mood. His serious demeanor was frustrating. I crossed my arms over my chest and looked at him.

"I'm listening," I said.

He ran his hand over the top of his hair and shifted on his feet.

"Lizzie, I think Freddie might be more into you than you think. I'm not interested in sharing your time with him. I know I had a dinner tonight but I never planned to leave you all night. I told you I wanted us to be together every day this summer. Why the hell are you here? Are you interested in Freddie?" he asked angrily.

"No!" I said incredulously.

He sighed, knowing that my outburst had to be the truth. I took his face in my hands and smiled at him.

"Teag, I'm just having fun. You had business and I understand that. Freddie realized I didn't have plans and invited me along. Now I'm being incredibly rude. Teagan, I'm your girl. Well, your girl for the summer," I said with a cringe. "But, babe, I'm hanging out with Freddie tonight," I said, pointing to the door. "So, if you want to hang out with me tonight, you are going to have to come back in and hang out with the both of us."

"Fuck that," he said.

"Fine, then go home and I'll meet you there by midnight," I said. I turned around and headed back into Joe's to continue Freddie's special night.

"Lizzie!" Teagan shouted. I turned around impatiently, but smiled when I saw he looked more relaxed.

"Lizzie, I'm going to The Littlest Bar to catch up with Cian," he said. "I'll either see you back here or at the apartment. If you need anything, just come find me, okay?"

I nodded and turned around to head into the restaurant.

When I got back to the table, all the guys were there talking and laughing. Freddie looked up to me with surprise then glanced behind me to see if Teagan was with me. I nodded at him and slid into the booth caddy corner to him. He studied my face, starting with my lips then flashed up to my eyes.

"Um, guys. I have to take off," Freddie said. "I told some friends I would meet them for drinks. I'll catch up with you soon."

After the guy sitting next to him got up, Freddie slid out. He held out his hand to me and I took it. He led me out the door and we walked several blocks away before he turned to me. He smiled.

"Want to finish the rest of that bottle?" he asked deviously. His eyes were so hopeful that I melted into his eagerness.

"It's your birthday night, Freddie. Whatever you want to do is up to you." I exclaimed.

We didn't talk about Teagan or what Freddie had said to me on the dance floor. He didn't try to move close but he was close enough for us to have an intimate conversation. I asked him about his college experience and if he had a lot of friends back home. He was most excited to talk about his family and described every sibling in detail. As I listened, I couldn't help but think about the fact that in one night, I knew more about Freddie than I did about Teagan after sharing his bed for three weeks. I didn't even know the names of Teagan's brothers, and wasn't sure if he had a sister. I tucked that away to ask him later. I felt bad that I hadn't even asked. Teagan knew way more about me than I did of him, and somehow that put a little knot in my chest.

"Lizzie?" he said, drawing me out of my thoughts. "We're here." He pulled my hand into his. There was no spark in our hand holding. There was no surge of passion like I had with Teagan. I looked at him as we walked to the apartment and wondered what would have happened if I had chosen him or if he did kiss me, like Teagan had assumed he was going to. No. He was a nice, attractive guy who I only saw as a friend. Yes, he may have the warmth and charm of a gentleman, but there was something so mysterious and untouchable about Teagan that sent shivers up my spine. Teagan was a little possessive and a whole lot in sync with my sexual desires. He put all his attention on me and never let me feel inadequate, until tonight.

Fourteen

Oops

Freddie and I stumbled into the dark apartment and I instantly went to the closet to grab the bottle and my guitar. When I went out to the living room, it was dark and Freddie was nowhere to be found. I turned to walk back down the hallway and he was standing just inside his door with his flexed arms holding the top of the door frame. He smiled and I noticed that he had put on some music.

"Let's listen to some of my music and see if you can play those songs," he said teasingly.

"Now that sounds like a dare," I said with amusement.

We sat down on the floor with our backs against his bed. He pulled out the two shot glasses and reached for the bottle. As we downed our shots, the warmth crept into my belly once more and we both turned and smiled at each other.

I pointed at his CD player and gave him a questioning look.

"Pure Gaelic music. Do you know how to dance to this?" he asked.

"Nah. I'm not sure I could keep up with the tempo," I said.

"C'mon. Let's give it a try. I'll lead," he said, standing and taking my hand.

Immediately, he had me bouncing through the room with fierce strides and all I could do was hold on. The room was spinning and I stumbled over my feet several times. We laughed and finally crashed to the floor. Ugh. I drank way too much. As I looked up to the ceiling, Freddie went and replaced the music with some Red Hot Chili Peppers. He grabbed two more shots and I sat up long enough to toss one back.

He lay next to me and we talked more about my family, my trip to Oregon, and eventually we were so piss drunk that all we did was laugh. When I looked up to see the bottle, it was empty. I immediately frowned.

"Oh no! It's all gone. Your birthday present is all gone," I said with a whiny voice.

"It's okay. I'll keep the bottle and the bag and always remember this birthday to be one of my favorites," he said with his arm propped up to look at me. He was so serious. I instantly froze. Was he really going to kiss me? I was so incredibly uncomfortable that I instantly looked back up at the ceiling and snorted really loud.

"Yeah, this was the best birthday evah!" I yelled with a fist pump.

We laughed so hard, I was crying. Rolling around on the ground, trying to stop laughing, we were interrupted with a huge clearing of a throat and an audible groan.

"Well, it looks like you guys finished that bottle," Teagan said from the doorway.

"Sorry, baby, we should have saved you some," I said as he came forward, pulling me to my feet. I was swaying and smiling at him. "Did you find Cian? How was your night? Did you get your drink on?"

"Oh yeah. Let's head to bed, okay?" he said. "Tomorrow, we're heading out to a real hurling match and we need some sleep."

"Okay. Bye, Freddie. Sweet dreams, birthday boy." As I looked back at him, his face looked solemn and he waved slightly. I sighed and was resigned that I did everything in my power to be a part of his great night. But instantly, I was entranced by Teagan and spending more time with him. Even though we only saw each other a few hours ago, I felt like it had been days since he touched me. I needed his touch. I needed the safety that surrounded me when he was with me. I needed him. And while I continued to tell myself this was a summer fling, I felt more and more for him every day. It was impossible not to. Deeply. I was starting to think I was in a little too deep. I wanted what I had with Freddie. I wanted to just be flirty with Teagan then have sex, of course. I wanted to go back to just days ago when we were carefree and not at all demanding. But tonight changed something in me. The way he was so possessive and mindful of my every move, the look of seriousness on his face. He felt more. I could see it. And maybe I thought I did, too. Fuck.

Teagan closed his door and told me that Cian had left to party with some of his other friends and wouldn't be back.

"We get to stay in the real bed tonight?" I asked excitedly.

He smiled and started for my clothes. I sighed then pulled off his shirt and unbuttoned his pants. While all of our clothes lay around us, we stood there looking at each other with electric warmth blazing between us. I touched his bare chest and moved my hand lower to find that he was ready for me. We instantly plunged for each other's mouths and didn't stop until I was flat on my back with him caressing every part of my body. He was powerful. He was forceful. The determined look in his eyes clearly said I was his. It was exhilarating, and I felt intoxicated on Teagan. No longer was I drunk by alcohol but his dynamic touches and the need to be complete with him. Wow. This was amazing. Fucking amazing.

He reached for a condom, and as we synced up, his kisses were all over my neck while he whispered how much he needed me, needed this. Before I could think, he completely took over. I just laid there as he plunged into me, our connection growing stronger with every thrust. When he finally stiffened and yelled out my name, I laid there completely wrecked. It was a whole new Teagan, one I had never seen before. And damn if it wasn't hot.

After several minutes of kissing my face, he withdrew and turned away to take care of the condom. I waited for him to come back. He looked down at himself and turned to me with alarm in his eyes. He looked distraught and I immediately sat up. I could feel it then. I scrambled to my feet and without caring one bit about my clothes, I ran to the bathroom and took the full, broken condom out of myself, trying to purge everything. I got wash clothes and water and peed. I showered and tried to extricate everything from inside me. I heard the door open and Teagan came in with only his boxers on.

As I brought the shower to a stop, I leaned out to grab a towel and he immediately grasped for it, getting into the shower with me. He dried every part of my body and kissed my wet hair. He whispered that everything was okay and he was sorry for being so forceful. I looked at him with a tear running down my face then smiled. "Oops," I said softly. "It's okay, Teag. We're good." Rationale hit me like a brick and I was uneasy. I don't know if it was from the sex or the condom breaking, but I never felt as dubious of anything in my life.

We headed back to bed and he put one of his tee shirts over me before we lay down, cradling each other until we silently fell asleep.

The next morning, I woke up to kisses being trailed down my bare neck. When I opened my eyes, I saw Teagan's head dipped towards the collar of my shirt. I sighed.

He looked up at me with adoration and whispered, "Morning."

"Hey. What time is it?" I asked. My head felt like someone had pumped it full of helium and it was about to pop. My mouth felt gross and my breath had to be awful since all I could smell was liquor.

"Dunno," he said as he continued to kiss my neck.

I looked over his shoulder to the window to gauge how high the sun was. It was up and it was blazing. It had to be almost noon. I popped my head up and groaned. God damn it. I threw myself back on the pillow. As I looked around the room, I noticed Cian was in his bed fast asleep.

I gave Teagan a questioning look as I rolled my eyes over towards Cian's side of the room. We never slept together when he was home, always opting to either snuggle on the couch or take the walk in closet on our sleep pad. Teagan shrugged and I smiled up at him.

"Hey, Teag? I have to talk to you about next weekend. An old friend is getting married up at Peak's Island in Maine and I have to go. I RSVP'ed before I met you and, well, I was planning on asking my friend, Shannon, to come with me. So, I won't be around from Friday until Sunday," I said, questioning his response after last night's debacle.

"I would like to go with you. When do we leave?" he asked with a knowing smile.

"Umm. Well, what time can you get off work on Friday? Summertime traffic up 95 is a bitch so I would like to leave earlier than later. The ferry runs all night but it really is a popular time of the year. It's tourist season," I said.

"I can see if they'll let me out at lunch." he offered.

"Perfect." I threw my arms around him and kissed his neck. "When is the hurling game today? We need a little hair of the dog if I'm going to sit through the blazing sun."

He grimaced at my announcement that I was terribly hung-over and said we would be picked up in an hour.

We showered together, washing each other's hair and smiling at each other when we brushed our teeth. When I walked out the door in a flowery sundress, Freddie almost ran into me. He looked like he had also just woken up. He gave a curt nod and headed into the bathroom. I stood there, stunned at his blatant attempt to avoid me. We had such a great night together and now it felt like there was an ice wall between us with that simple acknowledgement of my presence. I didn't know that would be the last time I saw Freddie until a week before the boys left for Ireland.

Fifteen

Hurl

When we made it to the game, we were already late. Of course, there was a pub on the sidelines so Teagan and I headed in alone and sat at a table for two. He watched the game from the window while I checked out the rest of the pub. There were hardly any women and I felt completely out of place. It was like Ireland suddenly transported itself to a place in Boston. So many of the patrons had thick Irish accents, like Teagan, but I could tell they weren't from the same location in Ireland. I recalled how everyone commented on my accent in Oregon at first.

I looked at Teagan and saw him smiling out the window. I relaxed back into my chair, and as I sipped my beer, I took in his rugby shirt and the fine lines of his face. He was at peace. I saw joy. I stared at him for a long moment, and when he glanced up, I looked at him questioningly.

"What is it, babe?" he asked.

"I want to know if you have a large family. I mean, I know you talk to your mom every week and I think I've heard you talk to your sister, but how many kids are in your family?" I asked.

Teagan clearly tensed. I didn't know why. It was a common question that most people asked on their first date, not almost six weeks into a friendship or whatever the hell we had.

He cleared his throat. "I have three brothers and two sisters. We aren't very close. I have a sister that is close in age, so she's great but my brother, William, is my favorite," he said with a smile.

I sat there, not saying anything, but nodding at his answer. I waited for him to say more but he didn't. He just looked back out to the field, and obviously someone had done something exciting because the whole pub erupted in cheers and slaps. I stayed in my chair and fingered the top of my bottle. When it quieted down, Teagan went to get us more drinks and we headed out to the bleachers to sit with his friends. There were beautiful men everywhere. The bleachers were filled with so much testosterone, I couldn't think straight. I couldn't even watch the game. I just watched the gorgeous men as they reacted to the game. I offered to become the gopher girl for drinks. Teagan handed me a bunch of bills and I shot off to the pub to grab a few more pints. When I made it to the bartender, he looked at me with a smile.

"Well, you're a sight for sore eyes," he said.

"Because I'm the only female in this entire place?" I asked, laughing. I ordered two beers and he handed me a shot of something too.

I eyed him quizzically, and I nodded a thank you before taking the shot.

. Every time I went to the bleachers, it became obvious that someone else needed a beer so I happily went back and forth to the pub. Every single time, the bartender gave me a free shot. The hair of the dog was making the previous night's hangover go away. I loved two day benders. Two hours later, I was so drunk, and the last shot he gave me had a napkin with his number on it. A hand came up behind me and took the napkin from my grasp.

I turned around and saw a very angry Teagan. Again. I smiled at him and took the napkin and tossed it back to the bartender.

"Sorry," I said. "I have a date tonight." The bartender pouted out his lip and I laughed.

Teagan grabbed my hand and led me out to the parking lot, plopping me in the back seat of the car. When he got in the car, he looked over at me with an amused smile. "Had a good time, baby?" he asked.

"The best hurling game I've ever watched!" I laughed. I was so wasted that when the other guys in the car laughed about something, I only rolled my eyes over in a haze, trying to catch up with what they were saying. It wasn't any use. My head felt heavy so I laid it down in Teagan's lap and he immediately combed his fingers through my hair while he continued to talk to his friends.

"Are you gonna fuck me when we get home?" I asked seriously.

He immediately looked down at me and his jaw dropped. Then, the laughter began. They were laughing so hard, I had to pull my head out of his lap because the shaking was making me sick. He pulled me tightly against him and kissed my forehead.

"Yes, love. You'll have whatever you want," he whispered in my ear.

Love? Did he just call me love? What a solid endearment for a summer fling. I smiled up to him and snuggled into his neck. At that point, I knew I loved Teagan. I loved him. But fuck it all to hell. That wasn't supposed to happen. But was it? We did start off casual, but now he was being possessive and caring. He was even calling me love. Maybe it wasn't so casual. Pushing the thought to the back of my head, I closed my eyes and blackness swept over me.

I woke up in a dark room with Teagan's hands wrapped around me. Saliva was pouring out of my mouth and I had to move. But I was stuck. My stomach started to come up my throat and I instantly pushed myself up, despite the dizziness, and stumbled frantically to the bathroom. The lid wasn't even up before everything came out. I could feel Teagan behind me, kneeling down, and then his hand started to rub up and down my back.

"No. Go. Away," I cried. Tears were streaming down my face and mixing in with the vomit coming out of my mouth. I couldn't let him see me like that. I was so embarrassed.

"No, baby, you're sick. Let me take care of you," he said in the softest voice.

He got up for a minute to get a warm washcloth and put it on the back of my neck. He continued to rub my back with one hand while he held my hair back with the other. When I turned to look at him, I could see he already had vomit on one of his hands. He smiled at me and gave me an endearing nod. That is when I got violently sick again. Good God. I thought I was going to die in that bathroom. I purged everything out and immediately put my face on the toilet, not caring that five guys put their asses there every single day. I laid there until I was consumed by sleep. I awoke to Teagan stripping off my clothes and gently putting me in the tub.

He had already drawn a bath for me and even put bubbles in it. He took off his boxers and got in behind me. He immediately rubbed the washcloth over me, cleaning every part of my body. He washed my hair with a cup and whispered sweet things to me about feeling better. He said everything would be better in the morning. When he was done, he put his hands around my waist and we stayed there until the water got cold. He dried me off and put me in one of his shirts then led me back to the bed where he caressed my wet hair until I finally fell asleep for the last time that night.

When I woke up, I heard noises coming from the kitchen. I looked over at the alarm clock and saw that it was ten thirty. Fuck. I missed my English class. Again. As I sat there and tried to figure out how many classes I'd missed, Teagan came through the door with a tray of eggs and toast.

"What are you doing here?" I asked, startled.

"I called in sick to work today. I was really worried about you, Lizzie. You were so drunk last night and I didn't want to leave you alone today," he said with concern.

I looked at him with a surprised smile. He placed the tray on my lap and told me to eat. I watched him as he sat at the end of the bed with a worn blue t-shirt and jeans. I took in my appearance. As I started to eat, he pulled my feet from underneath the covers and started to massage them. I groaned in delight and my head fell back to the wall.

"You didn't have to do this, Teag," I said. "Work is more important and you could have just called to check on me."

"I know but I needed to do this. I didn't realize how much you drank at the game," he said with a slight smile.

"I know, I know. I missed school this morning. I never should have taken so many shots. God, I'm so embarrassed. I feel like an asshole," I said.

"Don't say that, babe. We're going to take it easy this week. Maybe catch up on some sleep, eat a lot, and not go drinking. That way we can enjoy our trip to Maine this weekend," he said with a big grin.

"Yeah. I guess that sounds like a good idea. I just don't want to hold you back from having fun. This is your summer abroad and me getting drunk yesterday shouldn't affect you like this," I said sympathetically.

He shook his head. "No, I need this, too. We've done a lot over the past weeks, and a week without any drinking will be good. We can do things that regular couples do. I want to try out that Mexican restaurant you talked about and maybe go to the science museum. I'll pamper you and make you feel like a queen. Then, when we go to Maine, we can relax and enjoy ourselves with no dark circles under those beautiful eyes."

I smiled at him and took his hand into mine, intertwining our fingers.

"Now, finish your breakfast so I can climb back in bed with my American girl," he said with a squeeze. I placed the tray down on the floor and held my arms out for him.

Sixteen

Maine

By the time we packed my car on Friday afternoon, we had a great sobering week. We went to museums, movies, new restaurants, and hikes around the city. We held hands and cuddled when we stopped by coffee shops. We always stayed within a foot of each other when we were together. Teagan was doing well at work and I was able to catch up on my classes after only a few days and some long conversations with my professors.

Throughout the week, Teagan asked me questions about my friends who were getting married. I told him that when I was growing up, I always had a large crowd of friends, but after high school, everyone went their separate ways. One night over ice cream, Teagan asked me about Chase. I had mentioned him every once in a while but never went into the details of our relationship.

"Well, it's kind of a long story," I said. "Maybe I'll tell you about it on the ride up to Maine."

He smiled and simply nodded. I could tell he was looking forward to the upcoming weekend. I gave him a knowing smile, letting him know that I was also looking forward to our trip alone. Not to mention that we'd have my family's island cabin for two whole nights.

When we get outside to head out on the road, he started tickling me at the bottom of his steps. I started laughing out of control and he pulled my car keys out of my hand.

"Hey! What are you doing?" I asked aghast.

"Driving." he said with confidence.

"You don't even have a driver's license!" I squealed.

"Yes, I do."

"Humph." I offered no more protests. I felt much better sitting wingman, since I'd be able to enjoy the view. The view of Teagan.

We weren't even on the exit to North 95 when he glanced at me and asked, "So… Chase?"

"You remembered?" I asked in surprise.

"Yes, I want to know about your previous boyfriends. He must have been important if you were with him for a few years and moved across the country for him."

"Um. Okay. Well, Chase and I have known each other since my freshman year in high school. He is two years older than me. I actually was dating his friend, EJ, but that didn't last long, and Chase was kind of an asshole when EJ and I dated, like I wasn't good enough for his friend. It was really weird. So, I was a sophomore when I first went to a party and he came up to me and acted like he never hated me. It was so confusing. One minute, he hated me and then the next, he liked me. One minute, he looked at me like I was disgusting and then the next minute his eyes were looking me up and down like he wanted to swallow me whole."

"I can understand that need… to eat you up, I mean." He smiled at me.

"Nice." I laughed. "Well, anyway, that night, he made sure I got his pager number and told me to call him if I ever wanted a ride to school. I took the bus but my house was on his way to our high school. So, that Sunday, I paged him and he called me right away. He's friends with my brother and Conner loves him. So, that week, he started picking me up every day. He always had hard rock blaring through the radio so I could hear his truck coming down the road before he honked his horn."

"We remained friends and I started dating another guy, and even though I could tell he wasn't pleased, he still gave me a ride every day. After that, well, he graduated. He started going to a local college, and one night at a keg party, he and I sat in the back of his truck and reacquainted ourselves. He kissed me that night for the first time. It was nice," I said with a soft smile.

"After that, it was a full on relationship. We saw each other every day, and about a year later, he told me he accepted a job in Portland, Oregon. At first, I was a little panicked because I was going to lose him. I did want to travel. I had so many mixed thoughts about what I should do. I was scared to be alone and I loved him. I really did. After he watched me for a few minutes, he took my hands and said he wanted me to go with him."

"I wanted to get away and he talked about his apartment and the different things I could see there. He had me convinced that it wouldn't just be a temporary move but a life move," I said. "I didn't get very good grades in school because we partied. A lot. My parents were concerned about me not going to college and I could see the disappointment in their eyes. I couldn't bear it anymore, so when I told them I was moving to Oregon, they perked up like I was going to do something with my life," I said, air quoting the word "do." I laughed.

"We moved six weeks later and he was right. He was a whole different person. We met a lot of people, and a few of our friends even picked up and moved out there to be with us. We partied more than I ever had in my life. We both celebrated our 21st birthdays there and we were out of sight from our families and our neighborhood. I got a good job and did really well. I was an administrative assistant for three years at a good company, and

I think my parents were proud of me. They came out to visit and I took them to the local waterfalls and hot springs. They left me there, very satisfied that I was living a good life."

"One night, after Chase graduated from college, we decided to stay. Neither one of us saw a reason to move home. I had a decent job and he was able to get a really good job so we got a nicer apartment. It turns out that an apartment and a good job won't make a relationship work. One night, I brought up marriage and he flipped out. I think I noticed we had grown apart. At parties, we hardly hung out with each other. At the beginning, we couldn't keep our hands off each other, but it changed sometime. I don't know," I said as I looked out the window at the passing cars. I started to think about that fateful night when it all ended.

I would never tell Teagan about it. I didn't tell many people that didn't already know. I will never forget the look that Chase gave me when he found me out back, making out with one of his co-workers. Chase started calling me every name in the book. I will never forget the hurt in his voice. I will never forget when he threw all my stuff out of our apartment and onto the front steps. I will never forget living in my car for two weeks while I found a place to live.

"He and I went our separate ways and I decided that Oregon was the place that he wanted to be, not me. I didn't feel like I belonged there anymore so one day, about five months after we broke up, I decided to start my life over again and move back to Boston. You met me weeks after I returned," I said with finality.

He squeezed my hand over the clutch of the car and smiled. "He was a stupid guy to let you go," he said sweetly.

I pulled my hand away, feeling guilty, and put David Gray in the CD player. I immediately switched it to "This Year's Love" on purpose. His face went solemn and I quietly sang alone.

As we drove onto the ferry to the island, we locked up the car and went up to the passenger deck. It was a beautiful summer day. I loved the glistening ocean and the songs of the birds, hunting for their prey, and the great salted breeze. I leaned back and my whole body relaxed. Teagan could see the change in me.

"This place suits you," he said, smiling over at me. He drew close and we kissed. It got deeper, and by the time it ended, we were nearly at the island. I drew back and watched as the boat started to turn around to unload. I stood up and grabbed his hand. Everyone around us started whistling and clapping at our obvious public display of affection. He kissed the back of my hand lightly and we headed down to the car. I took the keys and gave him a funny look then stuck my tongue out at him. He chuckled and we got into the car.

"So, Teag, who was your girlfriend in high school? There must be a good story there," I said with a laugh.

"I dated someone for a while but things in Ireland are much different than in America. We went to the movies and occasionally kissed, but we never partied hard. I would walk her home from class and we held hands in school," he said with a smile.

"That sounds so tame. It doesn't seem like the Teagan I know." I laughed.

"Yeah, it wasn't cool to do what we just did on the deck at home. My mother and father would not be happy. And her parents? God, I don't even want to think about it," he said.

"So what happened?" I asked.

"Umm…we're still friends but we just grew apart, I guess. Kind of like you and Chase." He looked over at me, gauging my reaction.

I patted his knee, reassuring him that I understood.

"I'm glad you're here, Teag. You're about to enter island partying. It can kind of become insane, so watch out."

"I'll only be watching you." He smiled at me.

I gave him a cheeky smile and started the car out onto the ramp. Teagan was immediately rapt by the island and the people milling around, either getting off the ferry or people who were waiting for others. I drove up to the local store and turned off the car.

"Food. We need food. Then we'll head down to the docks to get some fresh lobsters," I said.

We grabbed burgers, hot dogs, chips, beer and water. Teagan threw down his credit card and I blushed.

"Why do you always pay for everything?" I asked, perplexed.

"Because you're my girl and no respectable guy lets his girl pay," he stated.

"Okay, then." The clerk smiled at Teagan and asked him where he was from. He smiled back to her and said he lives outside of Cork in Ireland. He grabbed the bags and my hand and we headed out the door. When I looked back at the young woman, she was entranced by watching Teagan. I couldn't blame her.

After we picked up the lobsters, we head towards the small cabin. It was painted blue and had a sun room set off to the right. Both the front door and the back door had beautiful window archways above them. Teagan looked at the cabin and then back to me.

"This is amazing," he said slowly under his breath.

I gave him a quick kiss on the cheek and leaped out of the car. I ran up to it and threw open the door to the familiar smell of summers lost to a younger version of me. Memories of the summers my family spent there came to life, and as I looked at the kitchen, I saw my dad in his jeans and t-shirt, reading a newspaper, while my mother hummed over breakfast. Teagan put his arms around my waist and he immediately started to kiss my neck.

"Let's get the groceries out of the car then I'll give you the ten cent tour," I said with a bounce in my step.

Teagan ignored me and started to look around the space while I brought in some bags. He turned to look at me and told me to stop. He flew out the door and grabbed the rest of our bags out of the trunk.

When he put down the bags and the food was put away, I leaned into him and wrapped my arms around his neck. His eyes locked on mine and he dipped down to kiss me. I turned my face and let him kiss my neck.

"That drives me crazy," I said, amused.

He chuckled.

"What do we do now?" he asked.

I pulled back and stared at him in earnest. "Well, we can rent bikes, go for a walk, or go down to the bar. We have kayaks and there's a baseball diamond down through the woods. We can play one on one," I said.

He cocked his eyebrow and I fake punched him in the stomach. One on one. God, his mind was always in the gutter. I started laughing and wiggled out of his arms and started out the back door. He chased after me and I headed for the forest behind the cabin. It took a quarter of a mile of dodging fallen trunks and the grassy dips through the forest until I came to the baseball diamond clearing. There were two small deer hiding out in the shadows. I stopped and gazed at them. Teagan laughed as he came up behind me.

I put my finger over my mouth to tell him to be silent. His eyes darted around the clearing and I saw when he finally registered the deer. His whole face lit up and he took my hand. He led me to the pitcher's mound and sat down with me in his lap. Flowers were blooming behind the diamond and I peered over Teagan's shoulder to see some people horseback riding on the nearby trails.

"Lizzie, what are you thinking about?" Teagan asked.

I put my head back to his shoulder and sighed.

"This is my peaceful respite," I said. "I'm whole here, and with you with me, it just feels so good."

"I know what you mean," he said as he placed a kiss on my temple.

I looked up at him with surprise. How could he possibly know what this place meant to me? He'd only been there for less than an hour and he loved this place as much as I did?

"No, it isn't about the place, Lizzie. It's you," he said. He ran his hand over his head then down his face, seeming to struggle with an internal battle.

"It's you," he continued. "You've become something more to me in these past few weeks. Coming here with you has made me feel different. I... I've never felt like this about anyone. You're one of a kind, Lizzie. You mean...a lot to me."

"You mean a lot to me, too. But I have to ask a question," I said. I didn't want to bring up the night of Freddie's birthday and the way he reacted to me being out with Freddie, and the way Freddie ignored me after that night. But I had to ask. It didn't make sense after the initial proposition of just being a summer fling. He made it feel like something more than that after that night, and I wouldn't know what he really thought unless I asked.

Teagan tensed behind me. I whipped around to look at him and he gave me a slight smile. He nodded for me to continue.

"Why were you so upset when I went out with Freddie last week?" I looked at him pointedly.

He shifted and his grip around me relaxed a little bit. I could see different feelings jump across his face but I couldn't make out his thought process.

"Dunno. I think Freddie likes you. I think he has since the first night we met you," he said.

"Are you... Do you think I like him, too?" I asked.

"Well, that night, I wanted you to be with me and you never expressed interest in him before. I thought maybe you were growing tired of me and I was worried I would lose you. I mean, not lose you because I know I am going to lose you. But I would lose this, here and now," he said as he put his hands over my shoulders.

"Teag, I like him. I like him like a friend. Sure, he's attractive but I've never felt anything for him. It has never been like it is with you. From our first kiss, I felt like you had a piece of me forever. I know that it's just a summer thing, but I won't ever forget this summer. I know that," I said firmly.

"I won't ever forget it either, Lizzie," he said as he nuzzled my neck.

Much later, we walked in the darkness through the woods, hand in hand, towards the cabin.

Seventeen

Romance

After a wonderful night of steamed lobster, beers, and christening of every piece of furniture in the cabin, Teagan and I slept in late. Even when we woke, I moved into his arms and we smiled at each other. We lay there for a long time, enjoying the complete silence of the island. I couldn't remember it being so quiet out there. The buzz of the city was long gone, and I could tell Teagan was enjoying the peace as much as I was.

I heard a large group of people approaching the cabin, and Teagan lifted an eyebrow at the noise.

"It's probably just a bunch of hikers. People don't really care about trespassers here. Everyone is going somewhere on the island," I said.

Just then, I heard the door open and the screen door slam shut, and all I heard were female voices. Wait... Oh my God. I heard Kelly first then Amanda and they were coming up the stairs singing, "Lizzie, Lizzie, baby." I shot straight up and pulled the sheet up over my naked chest. I looked over at Teagan and he looked amused.

When they got to the doorway, they looked in and I could tell they were going to immediately pounce on the bed. When they were startled by Teagan, they immediately backed up. I smiled at them. "Hey, girls. Long time, no see! I can't believe you're here," I exclaimed.

"Uh, hey, Lizzie. Girls, let's go downstairs and give Lizzie a few minutes to get dressed," Amanda said as she cocked an eyebrow at me.

My eyes snapped back to Teagan and he was still smiling at me.

"Your girlfriends, I take it?" He laughed.

"Oh God. Teag, I am so sorry," I said.

He waved his hand, and once the girls were downstairs, he lifted the sheet off his naked body and I watched him walk across the room to his bag to collect some clothes. He stopped to see if I was going to get dressed. His slightly confused look quickly turned to his usual amused smirk.

"Are you checking me out?" he asked.

"Always," I said unabashedly.

I threw on a robe and jumped off the bed. As I walked downstairs, all I heard was small laughter and murmuring. As I rounded into the kitchen, all my old girlfriends sat at the table with steaming mugs of coffee in their hands. Kelly pointed to an empty chair in front of a coffee cup and said, "Sit." She was fierce. Another red head in the crowd and this could get surly.

"Spill," they all said at once.

I shrugged my shoulders.

"His name is Teagan. He's here from Ireland for the summer. We met when he first got here and we're really close friends," I said, looking down at my perfectly made cup of coffee with sugar and cream and caramel drizzled over it.

I looked up to smile, and all their faces were blank. Kelly's mouth was wide open.

"Lizzie. That," she said as she pointed up to the bedroom, "is not just close friends."

I sighed.

"Girls, it can't go anywhere so I'm just having fun, and since we're all here together, can't we just relax? I haven't partied in over a week and I want to get down and dirty with my girls," I said, sipping my coffee like it would save me from the embarrassment of not knowing what the fuck was going on with Teagan and me.

"Hell yes!" Amanda screamed as she went over to the sound system and popped in a CD. I knew what she was doing. It was a tradition for us. Once, in sixth grade, there was a talent contest and we performed a choreographed dance to "Pump up the Jam." We all instantly fell into step in the living area space, pushing tables and chairs away to make room for all of us. Even though Kelly didn't participate in the original, we made sure that, over time, everyone knew the dance steps, and while some of them changed to make them a bit sexier, it was the official start up to a girl's weekend. I got in the front of the line and started my hips, falling into the rhythm of their heads bobbing in the back. It was very serious, like we were back in sixth grade and needed to win the grand prize, which we didn't. I was sure that the male a Capella group didn't have the same fun memories that we did.

As we turned in a circle to move my hips in a slow fashion, I saw Teagan staring at all of us like he had never seen a show before in his life. I could see his pride, the riveting stare, only on me. The song wound down and we all started laughing and hugging.

"And the commencement begins! Is Holly nervous about today?" I asked.

127

"Hell no," Amanda said. "She wanted to come with us but her mother-in-law is making her up and doing really strange things to her hair." The rest of us rolled our eyes.

"Lizzie," Teagan's voice came from behind me. "I don't think you've introduced us." He placed his hand on my back and looked around the girls expectantly. Their mouths opened and then shut again. I could tell they loved his accent as much as I did.

"So, Teagan, this is Amanda, Kelly and Sarah. They are very old friends. We went to school together. Girls, this is Teagan, my...my..." and just as I was going to say, friend, Teagan interrupted and said, "I'm Lizzie's boyfriend." He politely shook their hands while the flush of my skin was apparent. All the girls darted their looks between him and I while plastering smiles on their faces.

"Teagan, it's a pleasure to meet you. Any friend, umm, boyfriend of Lizzie's is a friend of ours. But are you sure you know what you're getting yourself into?" Amanda said with all seriousness in her face.

Shit, she wasn't going to bring up all the guys in my life, was she? I started to clear my throat, begging her to halt that thought. She gave me a wicked smile and put her hand on Teagan's arm.

"You'll never be able to keep up this weekend, so hold onto your knickers," she said with a laugh.

"I think I'll manage." He laughed while throwing his arm around my shoulder. I looked to him and smiled.

"Is that a challenge, Teag?" I asked.

"It's a promise, Lizzie O'Malley," he said with a mocking sneer.

"Okay, well, we have to go. If we're going to actually make it to this shin dig, we might as well doll ourselves up. Lizzie, do you need anything?" Kelly asked as she blatantly stared at Teagan.

"Nope, all set. Teagan bought me a beautiful outfit and we're psyched," I said with pride. Teagan squeezed my ass.

As I showed the girls out to the front lawn, I asked where they were staying. Apparently, Holly's family rented out the only hotel on the island for everyone to stay in. They were giddy with excitement. As we were hugging, I gave them a reassuring nod that I would see them later.

As Kelly hugged me again, she whispered in my ear, "Oh, and Lizzie, Chase is here with Tyler. He wants to see you."

My whole body tightened, and when I was about to ask her ten different questions, she rolled her eyes and headed off down the path to the hotel. I stood outside the cabin in my robe for who knows how long. What the fucking hell was Chase doing there? Sure, they were his friends too, but it was a major trip for one night of wedding debauchery. Why does he want to see me? What didn't we say on our trip from Oregon to Colorado? I always pushed marriage with Chase, trying to get my mind from racing about my place in life, or should I say, running away from life. I did want to settle, but after Chase's declaration of not being ready for that type of commitment, I knew. I knew we were over. That rejection was all it took for me to lash out and hurt him the way he hurt me. Sure, actions are hurtful, but after years of us being together and exploring life, his words of denial cut so deep, nothing made sense anymore. I felt lost. Now, I would see him again. In a few short hours, I would be in the same church with him, watching our friends marry. Fucking irony. I pushed aside the thought of him even being there, and decided to avoid him at all costs.

Teagan came out to the front steps with a mug in hand. When I heard the slam of the screen door, I turned to him and smiled brightly. His long cargo shorts with a million different pockets accentuated his bare chest and feet. He became more beautiful every day.

"Your friends are interesting." He smiled.

"Yeah, they are," I said as I rounded up to the sun room.

"You were standing on the green grass in that silk white robe, the sun shining through your red hair. God, you're a vision," he said earnestly.

I blushed and looked into his eyes, wagering if I should say anything about Chase. Fucking fuck.

"So… boyfriend?" I asked coyly.

"Yes. This weekend, we are just that," he said with finality.

I crumbled at his words. It was not safe. It was not the truth. He was not mine. Could I pretend? Wasn't I doing that every single moment I spent with him? This was me, though. High drama in the most messed up situations. Sometimes I wondered if they should do a Lifetime movie about my consistent screw ups. With Chase on my mind and the thoughts of only being Teagan's girlfriend for a weekend, I started to cry. Teagan wrapped his arms around me and shushed me.

"What did I say? Why are you upset?" he asked.

"Because you and I both know the truth, Teagan. We will never be. You leave and I lose," I said through my tears.

He looked at me with sympathy and nodded. "I lose too," he whispered.

There was nothing more to say. We just stood there, hugging each other and letting the reality set in.

As Teagan and I dressed for the wedding, I glided through the rooms, applying small amounts of makeup and blow drying my hair. When I pulled out the dress from the garment bag, Teagan came up behind me and led me to a full length mirror in the master bedroom. He helped me step into the black spaghetti strap dress. Pulling up the zipper, he put both of his hands on my shoulders and gave me a quizzical look.

"What?" I said.

"Something is missing," he said.

"No, you saw this dress on me at Filene's and this is the same dress," I said, poking him in the chest.

"Hmmm…"

I turned back around to look at myself in the mirror and it was a welcome sight. I looked beautiful. I saw my radiant tan from the hurling Saturdays and hikes with Teagan. I saw the weight I'd left my parents house. Food seemed to be the last thing on my mind this summer. Teagan pulled a chain out from his pocket and unclasped the necklace. He put it around my neck and my hand immediately went to the Claddaugh charm. I stilled and felt nothing but shock. All the breath left my lungs as I clutched the very romantic gift in my hand. Was he telling me something with this gift? Was I now his girl for real or just the temporary one that he initiated at the beginning of the summer? I shook my head and pushed the thought of a real relationship to the back of my head. Teagan would never know what some necklaces meant to American girls.

I turned to look at him and he gave me the sexiest smile. "For my American girl. So you never forget your Irish boy," he said quietly.

"It's beautiful," I said in awe.

"I'm glad you like it," Teagan said, putting his forehead to mine. "I'm glad you like me."

He kissed me softly, and as soon as it started, it ended. He crooked his head towards the outside window and said, "Let's go, baby. We don't want to be late."

I nodded, slipped on my new strappy black heels, and grabbed my clutch. He held out his hand. I took it and we headed out towards the car.

Eighteen

Dance

When we pulled up to the parking area of the expansive house that overlooked acres of land, I was automatically sent back ten years. Familiar faces sat on the back of cars, drinking beers and laughing with each other. My old friends were crazy. They saw any event as a drinking event, always prepared with coolers and hatchbacks to chill out on. They probably had been here for hours...A few of the guys I ran with saw me in the passenger side and started shouting. Suddenly, my car was swarmed and my friend, Jack, pulled me out of the car. He lifted me out of the seat and spun me around while placing a kiss on my cheek. People started to move towards me but my head jerked up to find Teagan. I held up my hands to my friends and walked around to Teagan's side, opening his door. He looked up to see me beaming at him. As he grabbed his dress coat, I shook my head.

"You won't need that here. My friends don't really do dress code. I'm sure there are many in baggy shorts and flip flops. Better yet, take off the tie, too. Get comfortable."

I pulled him out of the car and we headed around to the trunk, where Amanda, Kelly and a dozen other people waited to say hello. Amanda took over the introductions with Teagan while I had a chance to chat with people I hadn't seen in years. The new hair styles, the new tattoos, and the new people on their arms were a lot to take in. I knew that one night wouldn't be enough to catch up with everyone. One of my best pals, Sean, sauntered up to me and cried out, "Lizzie Lou!"

"Oh my God!" I screamed and ran into Sean's tattoo covered arms and kissed him on the mouth.

"Now that's what I'm talking about," Sean said. "It's been forever, Liz. You look so beautiful and I've missed you like crazy."

I smiled at him and we both just stared at each other, trying to take in each other's features. Two old friends that had been to hell and back together and yet there was never any chemistry. We knew it from the beginning when we started rating horror movies and laughed about our burps over beer. We were instantly friends. No more.

Teagan came up beside me and cleared his throat.

"Oh, fuck, Teagan. This is Sean, one of the most incredible friends I've ever had. Sean, this is my friend, Teagan. He's visiting for the summer from Ireland," I said, shaking my head at the amazing feeling I had about seeing him. It was the most perfect day. Sean was there and Teagan was meeting him.

They shook hands and Sean turned to me, giving me a wink.

"Sit next to me. Wedding ceremonies put me to sleep and I know that sitting with you will make it so much more fun." He laughed, turning his beer up to take a swill.

"You bet!" I said just as Teagan put his arm around me. Feeling a bit uncomfortable around the guy I'd known for over ten years, I looked to him and said, "But only if you give me one of those!" I pointed to his beer. He handed his to me. Then he leaned into my ear on the opposite side of Teagan and whispered, "I backwashed just for you, Lizzie Lou." I laughed and finished the beer in four swallows.

Something else caught Sean's attention and he winked at me again as he walked away. I turned and studied Teagan's face.

I held up my hands and said, "Truly! Only friends. He's like a brother to me."

He smiled, knowing I could read his face. He took my hand and we headed towards the church that adjoined the land to the house. It was a pretty white church, set right on the beach. There was nothing fancy about it except the land it sat on. There were no stained glass windows. There was a small door and very uncomfortable looking bench seats. It reminded me of a church from the Civil War. Surely, the building was a fire disaster waiting to happen, but the people on the island kept up with the paint and the cleaning. The immaculate grounds were amazing.

"It's lovely here," Teagan murmured, tearing me away from my thoughts about the church.

"It is. Are you nervous? There are a lot of people I know here and you don't know anyone. I hope it doesn't take away from my time with you tonight. It's just so great to be around my people after so many years." I smiled.

"Lizzie. I'm not nervous. I'm here for you and we'll have our time together later tonight and all day tomorrow," he said as he swept his hand across the necklace he gave me.

I sighed and kissed him on the cheek. "Thanks for understanding."

Amanda and Sean swept by us, and Sean immediately took my hand to head into the church. He took us up all the way to the front and we took seats in a loud clatter. Teagan sat next to the aisle and Sean was on my right. Immediately, he jumped in to make a funny joke about the old woman playing the organ.

"Why are all organists so old and…" I cut him off by slapping his leg.

"Dude, you can't criticize a woman who obviously has a talent for something and enjoys it," I said.

"Oh yeah? What's your talent?" Sean asked.

I snickered at him and Teagan leaned over me and quietly said, "That isn't something we should speak of in a church."

Sean and I busted out laughing, and as the wedding party started down the aisle, I could only look back once because I was laughing so hard. Then the organist started to sing and, sadly, she didn't have a talent for singing. Sean and I were trembling, tears running down our faces while we tried to remain composed throughout the short ceremony. Teagan just shook his head and smiled at us. I couldn't understand why he wasn't laughing as hard as we were. Maybe it was just that Sean and I were back to our normal selves, laughing about everything and anything in life.

As we dried our tears, we stood to clap for Holly and Ben. She gave me a stern "You suck" look and I laughed at her while blowing her kisses. As we headed out to follow them, Teagan put out his elbow and I took it, thinking how much of a gentleman he was. He whispered something to me but my face was immediately locked onto Chase's. He was staring right back. He flicked his gaze to Teagan, and I turned back to him, asking him to repeat what he just said. He looked at me with a confused look and tried to see what I was looking at. I obviously had reacted to Chase's face, and Teagan's concerned look made it so uncomfortable, I couldn't breathe. I felt a panic attack coming on, so I pulled him back to my car, where I pulled a beer from the trunk and downed the whole thing.

"Lizzie, what's wrong?" Teagan asked.

"Oh, weddings, you know," I said, waving him off.

"Well, no, I don't. You look pissed or something," Teagan pressed.

"Pissed? Far from it. I just laughed my ass off for fifteen minutes straight while a good friend got married. I hardly even heard the ceremony," I said, laughing.

"Ah. Yes, well, it was just the traditional vows," he said, grabbing a beer.

"Okay, let's hit the food," I said.

I didn't see Chase again while we ate. White linen tables were arranged with votive candles as centerpieces and the slight breeze of the ocean made the white tents look like a huge flash light. It was gorgeous. Holly had taken simple and made it priceless. We watched the couple dance and cut the cake. The toasts were ridiculous and there were quite a few F bombs laced throughout them. Obviously, people were as toasted as we were. Sean leaned in and asked if I wanted to smoke a joint. I shook my head. I wasn't going to get totally blitzed. I wanted to savor every moment.

Teagan twisted to me and sweetly presented his hand. "Dance with me?" he asked as he kissed my hand. The beginning of Counting Crows' "Round here" was coming out of multiple speakers throughout the tent and rose to follow him to the makeshift tiled dance floor. I smiled at Holly as Teagan drew me close, putting his forehead on mine.

"I like this band," I said.

"I know. You were wearing their shirt on our first certified date." He smiled.

"Date?" I asked with a mocking smile.

"Yes, Lizzie. We've been dating," he said softly.

I sighed. "I don't date, Teagan. We are more than just dates. Shit, I basically live with you and the guys."

"Good point." He chuckled and drew me closer with his hand on the small of my back.

We danced through half the song when I heard Chase's voice come from behind me.

"May I cut in?" Chase asked.

Teagan popped his head up with surprise. He looked at me with a "Do you want to?" face.

"Chase," I said leisurely. "Please don't."

Teagan's features altered into a look that I'd never seen before. He was obviously shocked but more defeated. He let go of me, like I had burned him, and Chase immediately jumped in to take over the dance.

"That was a shit move," I said, keeping my distance from him. He and I were not together, and everyone, including Teagan, needed to comprehend my body language.

"Who is he?" Chase asked firmly.

"What does it matter to you, Chase?" I said, finally looking up at his face.

"Just fucking answer the question," Chase said with impatience in his words.

"He's a friend. My boyfriend," I said, thinking about how Teagan had claimed me for the three days on the island.

"Well, that was fast!" Chase scoffed.

"It isn't like that. He's from Ireland and he's going home at the end of the summer, and now I don't know why I'm explaining this to you," I said, squirming from him. I just wanted to find Teagan and explain that I didn't know Chase was coming. I felt…guilty. But was I supposed to feel guilty about being with Teagan while Chase was there and not the other way around? All those years I spent with Chase suddenly meant nothing and as each minute ticked by, I was losing Teagan. I had to find him.

Chase pulled me closer with force.

"Lizzie. I need to talk to you. Please just give me five minutes and you can go back to your date. I'm not going to ruin your night," he said softly.

"You already have. He knows about you, Chase. I'm sure he's not happy right now." I scowled at him.

"Just listen," he said softly, pulling me close as the song changed to another that I couldn't even comprehend because my head was swimming with a million thoughts.

"I need a drink," I said and walked off. Chase was on my heels, and when we made it to the keg, he grabbed two red plastic cups and tapped us both a beer.

As I started to drink, he cocked his head to the side and motioned me to follow him. I turned to survey the tent for Teagan. He was nowhere. He didn't leave, did he? Good God, did Chase fuck everything up?

I stepped five paces into the dark, grassy space and Chase turned around.

I tapped my foot and said, "I'm listening. Why are you here?"

"Lizzie, I miss you. I know that I wasn't ready for marriage, but since I left you in Colorado, I've been so...so unhappy. Even when we were broken up, you were still there in Portland and I knew I'd still see you. But you're gone now and I've had so much time to think. You've been everything to me for years. I need you. I want to make you happy and, I will do anything, and I mean anything, if you would just come home with me. I'm begging you. You can go to school there and we can get a nicer apartment. I know things won't be the same, but I'll spend the rest of my life trying to undo what I did when I said I couldn't commit to you." He pleaded with ferocity. He was like an animal, walking around his prey, ready to pounce.

I stood there, astounded. Holy fucking hell. I must have stood there for at least five minutes while I watched him squirm under my scrutiny. My knees started shaking. Was it Chase or the sea breeze becoming colder? My palms were sweaty, so I handed Chase my plastic cup then wiped my hands down my black dress.

"You look so beautiful," Chase said.

"Chase," I said with resignation.

"Just tell me you'll think about it. Just tell me you'll look back and remember all our good times and the better times we can have in the future," he said.

I could feel Teagan behind me before I saw Chase's face turn into surprise. I grabbed my cup from Chase's hand and stood there.

"Are you okay?" Teagan asked.

"No," I said.

"What can I do?" Teagan asked in concern.

"You can get me the hell out of this conversation," I said fiercely.

"Lizzie," Chase said, trying to grab for my hand.

"I wouldn't do that if I were you," Teagan warned.

"What is she to you? She's just your cheap fuck, right? Like you really know my Lizzie." Chase scowled.

Teagan laughed. I turned to look at him, wondering what he thought was so funny.

"It seems to me that you lost the right to know her intentions when you promised not to marry her after treating her like a cheap fuck for years," Teagan said.

Teagan took my arm, and as we walked back to the tent, he turned to Chase and said, "Oh and she isn't *your* Lizzie anymore."

"Lizzie! Promise me you'll think about it. When he leaves you, you'll be alone. I'll always be here for you, baby. Think about it… about us," Chase pleaded.

We walked away and I didn't see Chase again that night.

Nineteen

Thoughtful

As Teagan and I headed back to the tents, his arm tightly centered on me. I looked down at my empty cup. I frowned and said, "I think I need something a bit stronger."

He nodded and we went up to the bartender. He bought us each a Seven and Sevens, my favorite drink. He handed me one and I sipped off it, closed my eyes, and thanked God that the conversation with Chase didn't ruin my evening with Teagan after all. He was tending to me, making sure he got the jabs in that I couldn't, and buying me my favorite drink. He knew me so well, and yet, I couldn't bring myself to look at him. I didn't want to see the anger, or hurt, or jealousy that he had that night I went out with Freddie. I needed to reassure him that I wasn't involved with anyone but him.

"Lizzie.., fucking look at me." Teagan startled me and I immediately opened my eyes.

"There she is," he said with a smile. "I've been saying your name. Did you not hear me?"

"No. I just didn't want you to think that, you know, I was trying anything with Chase. It was a surprise. I didn't know until this morning that he was here on the island. I guess he didn't want me to know," I said, pleading with my eyes.

"I was listening the whole time. The whole time you were dancing, getting your beers, and standing off to the side, I was listening," he said without any regret in his eyes.

"Really? Teag, that's a bit creepy," I said, smiling.

"I know, but when I heard your voice, the pain when you said his name, I knew I couldn't leave you alone with him. He has some nerve to just show up and demand your undying love." He shook his head.

I placed my hand on his chest and drew closer to kiss him softly. It was such a tender moment as he wrapped one arm around me, making sure not to spill our drinks, and whispered David Gray song lyrics in my ear. As I leaned into him, he reassured me that everything would be alright and I was a strong woman, the strongest he'd ever met, and nothing could make me more special.

"Other men see it too, Lizzie. You have something that makes guys bat shit crazy. Maybe it's that you don't take shit from others. Maybe it's because you have fun and never look back on your regrets," he said.

"If you only knew how far from the truth that statement is. It would be laughable if it wasn't so sad," I said.

I downed my drink and took his full one, pulling off it. I was getting hammered and nothing was going to stop me. The girls were in the middle of the dance floor in a circle that was only meant for ladies. I handed Teagan back his drink and smiled devilishly at him before I headed straight to my oldest and dearest friends. They screamed and we danced to Bjork. She was an old time favorite of ours. Sexy and seductive. A beat that could make anyone move. I looked over to see Teagan watching me with a smirk on his face. I could tell that the last twenty minutes were over in both of our minds and I was so fucking happy for that. After many sweaty dances, I bowed out of the girls' dance circle and headed for the bar. Teagan was there instantly with bills in hand, buying me another drink. We took off outside the tent and went to sit on the grass, looking out to sea.

143

"Hey look, there's Ireland," I said, laughing.

Looking out at the open Atlantic Ocean, I thought about how far Ireland really was and I got sad. Sure, Oregon was probably almost the same distance but it felt close in my heart. I could close my eyes and see Burnside's busy street and Mount Hood overlooking the city. I couldn't envision Ireland at all, except through the man sitting next to me. He was Ireland. Any flag, any striped shirt with an emblem on it, every Irish accent in any movie would always be Teagan. It almost made me not want to go there ever.

"I really think it is much farther than the horizon from here." He chuckled.

"Do you think you'd ever want me to visit? I mean, my family goes there every few years to see our great, great aunts or who knows but I've never been. I can't envision what it looks like. I can only see you going in and out of college doors and hurling."

"It would mean a great deal if you came to visit me, Lizzie. I would like you to see the small town my family lives in and show you around Cork."

"Really?" I said with surprise.

"Really. I'll look into it when I get back and when I've made enough money to buy your tickets. We'll pick the perfect time, when I'm on holiday, and then we can spend some time together. My parents are very traditional so we'll sleep in different rooms but maybe a few nights, we can go to a bed and breakfast," he said with a devilish smirk.

I squeezed his side and felt the tears start to burn from the sides of my eyes. I would miss him and I knew short trips would never make a real relationship but if that was all I could get from Teagan, there was no way I'd ever say no. I looked at him and smiled. We headed back into the tent to dance again. Drinking and dancing made up the last few hours, and as I said tearful goodbyes to all my friends, I felt Teagan's warm hand rub up and down my back, assuring me that goodbyes weren't forever and I wasn't alone.

The hardest goodbye was to Sean. I saw him across the parking lot and sped off in my sandals, only to fall flat on my face, scraping my knees and crying out in pain. Teagan picked me up and held me as he looked over my injuries.

"Can you walk?" he asked in concern.

"Yes, Jesus. I just want to say goodbye to Sean. Dammit. Did he leave already? I don't know when I'll see him again," I said, crying my eyes out.

Teagan wiped away my tears and told me that it would be soon. "Sean's a good lad. We talked a lot about you tonight and he's a great friend."

I looked over his shoulder to see that Sean had gotten into Amanda's car and they were already driving off. I heard music and screaming coming from their car and I smiled. Crazy fuckers. I would see them again soon. I'd make it a point to reacquaint myself with them after the summer. They were my second family and time wouldn't keep us apart. They were true friends and would never possibly hurt me. They could always make me laugh and we would always be partying. I knew that escape would be needed once I lost the man in front of me.

"Lizzie!" Teagan snapped his fingers in front of my face. "You keep doing that."

"Doing what?" I asked as I swayed to my good knee.

"You keep going off to a faraway place when we're talking. There's something going on up there. What is it?" he asked.

"I can't help but think about when you leave. I think about all the great friends I have and how I take for granted that they live close enough for me to see anytime yet I never see them. With you, you'll be gone, and quite honestly, I'm afraid it won't be the same. You mean something different to me than they all do." I couldn't fucking believe I was spilling my guts out to him after we said this would just be a summer fling. I was getting way over my head, and while I put on a brave face and pretended that he was just another guy to me, it wasn't true. The alcohol was making me spit out shit I shouldn't have been saying. I'd scare him off. He told me not to fall in love with him, not to get attached, but how the fuck could I do that when he consumed every moment and every thought. He wasn't just a summer fling. He was someone that treated me with more respect, and something that resembled love, than I'd ever felt.

"Lizzie, it'll be okay. We'll stay in touch. At the end of the summer, we'll do what needs to be done. I have to finish school and you have to get back to your life. We'll know how precious this time has been but we'll also know that it'll be impossible to stay as we are."

"Yeah, I know. I'm just a little drunk, and having my friends around tonight really made me think of the past and how I'll never get back the time lost. Sometimes I feel like I wasted all those years in Oregon. My close friends are in my past but I want them here in my present too. I know my feelings for you will be stronger after you leave, Teag, and I'm afraid of that longing already."

Just then, a little girl walked by, holding her father's hand. She was probably three years old with long, curly blonde hair. She was crying so hard that it was hard to hear her father's shushes.

"I want to cry just like her," I said.

Teagan got in front of me and laughed. Then, he bent his head down to my forehead and said the most amazing words.

"You don't know how beautiful, adorable, and sexy you are. Inside and out. You show me your feelings and your fears and it makes you all the more irresistible. If you ever cried that hard, it would rip me to pieces. I hope I never have to see that," he said with a soft, gentle voice.

I leaned in and kissed him with so much passion, I thought I'd start sobbing right then. What the hell was wrong with me? I was crying about everything. His words, seeing Sean, leaving friends. But one thing I knew, I was not crying about Chase.

When our kiss broke, he pulled a red rose from behind his back and tucked it behind my ear.

"An Irish rose for my American girl," he said, pulling me to the car before driving us back to the cabin.

We spent the remainder of the weekend biking around the island, getting ice cream at the local cream shop, and listening to Sunday's Reggae Fest down at the docks. It was comfortable and we didn't waste a moment on the water. It was such a respite from Boston. When we headed back on the ferry to go home, we didn't go up on deck. We just stayed quiet and listened to music in the car. I could feel our relationship coming to an end. It was clearly the end of our pretend couple weekend as boyfriend and girlfriend, and I knew he could feel the distance, too. It was only July, but I knew we were over. The ride home was easy and quiet. By the time we got back to the apartment, Teagan and I scrambled to his bed and lay there, looking up at the dark ceiling, saying nothing. We didn't have sex that night but held each other like it was the last thing we'd ever do.

Twenty

Sobering Up

Monday morning came too early and I awoke to Teagan putting his tie on. I looked at him and winked. He smiled but it didn't reach his eyes. I stirred and sat up to see what was obviously wrong. He could tell that I noticed the change in his demeanor.

"I'm so tired. I don't know why. We had so much sleep and relaxation," Teagan said as he leaned over and kissed me on the forehead.

"I'm tired, too." I sighed. "I need to get up and head out to school." Teagan shook his head.

"Just wait until the other lads are done showering and out of here before you get up," he said as he looked down at his watch. "You still have time to get a little more rest."

I couldn't rest anymore. I was wide awake. Why was he so worried about me going out amongst the other guys? Was I not supposed to spend the night?

I looked at him with a blank face. "Are you upset with me, Teag?"

"No, baby, not at all. I just want you to get rest after a long weekend with your friends." He leaned down and fingered the necklace he gave me.

"Okay, Teagan. So I'll see you after work?"

"Yes. Be here at six. I have a late meeting," he said as a matter of fact.

"Sure, no problem."

He nodded and squeezed my arm. When he walked out, he didn't look back at me with his usual dazzling smile. Just firmly shutting the door behind him.

I was instantly on guard. Something was really wrong. There was a subtle shift in his mood. Teagan was not the Teagan I knew up until that point. Did he just shut me out? What the fucking hell just happened? He looked the part, he tasted the part, but it was faked. I knew it deep in my bones, and my first thought came in a wave as the hairs rose on the back of my neck. Flight. He won't hurt me as long as I don't get too involved. Holy fuck, I was already too involved. It's time to back off.

Three hours later, I headed out of my class, walking to my car in a haze. After a blissful weekend and an uneasy morning, I couldn't help but feel like the biggest loser in the world. I drove home and found Conner out front on the phone, waving his arms in clear frustration. I overheard two words. "Fuck Darcy," before I headed into the front door and up to my room. I fell on my bed and curled into a ball. A few moments later, the front door slammed and Conner was cursing loudly. His feet pounding up the stairs startled me and I prayed he wasn't coming towards my door.

When my door flew open, I could tell he was not only angry but pained.

"Conner, what's wrong?" I asked in concern.

"It's nothing. Darcy and I broke up because we can't see each other very much after the accident and well, it's tough," he said gruffly.

There was nothing I could say because I knew deep down, I was the reason that happened. Darcy and Conner were glued together when I came home from Oregon and I could see the way she looked at him. Conner got that look from a lot of girls at his shows but he never gave them the time of day when he was with Darcy. I guess she had captured his heart a little bit too.

"It doesn't matter. I have too much going on anyway. I wouldn't have any time with her," he said.

"Conner, I'm sorry," I murmured. "I… I…"

He waved his hands at me and smiled, giving me a brotherly look of love.

"Look, I know you've been going through a hard time since the accident, too," he said. "You're important to me, Lizzie. We're all worried about you and I know that you take a lot of the blame for that night. Darcy explained what she remembers and she said you did try to fight with her not to drive."

"But I failed."

He shook his head and walked to my bed, wrapping me up in a big hug. I half hugged him back. The phone rang from across the room on my dresser and Conner pulled back.

"O'Malley residence," he answered.

"Hold on a minute." He looked to me. "Teagan is on the phone," he said as he put his hand over the receiver.

I slowly shook my head back and forth.

"She's in the shower. Do you want to leave a message?"

He muttered a few more things while I ignored his end of the conversation, lying back down on my bed.

He hung up and asked, "What's up with that guy?"

"Not much. He's just a friend. He went to Holly's wedding with me. He's probably just checking that I got home safely."

"Well, he wants you to call him back," he said, brushing off something on his shirt.

I nodded and he gave me a curious look before he left my room. Minutes later, he started strumming his guitar and singing a song I'd never heard before. His voice put me into a trance. I closed my eyes, succumbing to sleep. Sleep had always been a way of escaping a place that I felt was too consuming. My dreams have always been vivid because of my racing thoughts to escape and be something different. That day, I only dreamt of Teagan. We were in a bar in Ireland where he introduced me to all of his family and friends. He dragged me around the city and we were happy. I felt more settled than I ever had.

Waking up to the phone ringing was a horrible disaster. I didn't want to wake up from that dream. It was the first in a long time that I finally found peace in. As I threw my legs over the bed, I noticed my nose was completely stuffed, I had a headache, and I felt like throwing up. Damn. I was getting fucking sick. I fucking hated feeling sick. I couldn't smoke, I couldn't drink and I couldn't escape the racing thoughts in my head of everyplace I would have rather been than in bed. The phone stopped ringing as I headed to the bathroom. My mom came up the stairs and handed me the phone.

"There's some nice Irish boy on the phone," she said with a glorious smile. My parents have always been big fans of Ireland and their partial connection to the land.

"Mom, what time is it?" I winced.

"Um...eight pm," she said, looking up from her watch. "Are you feeling okay, honey? Oh gosh, I hope you aren't getting what Conner had last week. I thought it was just the stress of finals," she said with concern.

I took the phone from her and answered. "Hello?"

"Lizzie, where are you?" Teagan asked. I heard laughter and music in the background and a sudden urge to throw up made me toss the phone down and race to the toilet. I threw up everything I had in me, which wasn't much, and started dry heaving, like my body wanted to rid itself from any future food as well. My mom gave me a warm cloth over the back of my neck.

My mother cleared her throat and put the phone up to her ear. "Hi there. I am sorry but Lizzie isn't feeling well right now, so she will have to call you back." After a long pause, I heard her continue to talking for several minutes as she walked back downstairs. Did she just laugh at something he said? God, he was good. Always the charmer.

After flushing the toilet and brushing my teeth, I felt well enough to dress in a sweater and yoga pants before crawling back to bed. I couldn't keep my temperature right the entire night, and as I fell into a restless sleep, I hoped to get back to the dream of Teagan and me in Ireland, in love and not in this limbo hell that was starting to wear me down. In love? Oh God! I loved him. I was in love with him. I wanted him.

Days flew by in a blur. Mom took some time off to be home with me. She helped me with the B.R.A.T. diet and soothed my back every time I threw it all back up. Teagan kept calling and was starting to get really worried because I wouldn't go to the phone. I didn't know how I felt talking to him now that I knew I had fallen for him. My guard was up and I knew that he could tear it down with just one word. I didn't want to be a bitch so I asked her if he was sick too and she shook her head. Wednesday afternoon, the phone rang and since I felt a little better, I jumped off my bed to answer it.

"O'Malley residence," I said.

"Lizzie. Are you okay? How are you getting on? I've talked to your mother more than you these past few days," Teagan said frantically.

"Teag, I've been really sick. I caught something from Conner. He had this exact same thing last week and, well, I guess it's my turn. I'm feeling much better though. I think the worst part is over. It must be the 48 hour bug or something."

"Ah, good. Then, we'll see each other tonight? Remember I told you I'm heading to New York City with Cian this weekend, right?" he asked.

"Um…" I put my fingers to my temples. "Yeah, sure. Big Apple. That should be fun for you guys. You'll love the Empire State Building, The Twin Towers, and Statue of Liberty."

He laughed in my ear. "Lizzie, am I going to see you before I go? It's been two nights without you. It's cold here," he whispered seductively. I could tell he was smiling. Double shit. The guard was officially down. Take it easy, Lizzie. Play it cool.

"I don't know about tonight, Teag. I'm still not feeling very well."

"Well, can I come to your house? I'll make you some soup and we can listen to music. Your guitar is still here. I can bring it to you," he said, slightly pleading.

"How will you make it out here?" I asked, thinking of the long T ride and the three mile walk.

"I'll take the T. I can be out there in a hour." he asked.

"Teagan, this flu is…" I started.

"Lizzie, I don't give a shit about the flu. Just let me come out and see you. I told your mom that I'd like to have dinner with them sometime, so I'll come to you," he said.

"Fine, but don't forget that I warned you." I smirked.

"See you in an hour then," he said then hung up, probably so I couldn't protest.

An hour later, I shivered, despite the 80 degree weather and waited on my front doorstep for Teagan to show up. I really couldn't understand his urgency to see me but it was giving me the butterflies. I did not want him to know I went and fell in love with him when he specifically told me not to. I watched the yellow cab pull up to the front of the house and I stood to watch him gather his black duffel bag out of the back. After he paid the driver, he turned and stood there watching me stand there, watching him back. Slowly, he walked towards me. His eyes never left mine.

"You look beautiful," he said.

"You're a fucking liar," I retorted.

He smiled as I started towards the door. Back in my house, I made the introductions between Teagan, Conner. my mother and father. Dad was away on a business trip and had just gotten back that day. He was pleased to see I was making new friends. They sat and talked for a little while. I just stayed at the kitchen table with my head over my crossed arms, watching them chat easily. It was nice that Teagan was there. I'd been in his world for so many weeks that I never thought he'd want to get to know mine. But this wasn't my world. This was just the house I grew up in and the family I ran home to at the age of 23. Unsettled, I stood up and took Teagan's hand, leading him up to my bedroom.

I lay down on my bed and he sat at the end of it, taking off my sneakers and rubbing my feet. I moaned. God, I missed his touch. His presence was so absent that I never realized how powerful it was. I thought about every time we had sex, and how I took it for granted. Every time he held me, I didn't pay attention to the zings that went through my body. It was probably because I was drunk almost every time it happened.

He got up on the bed and spooned me from behind, whispering how much he missed me over the last few days and how he was so glad to finally have me back in his arms. I listened to him talk, and as I felt the zings of his hands caress my shoulders, arms, waist, and ass, I fell into a deep sleep. There was no reason to dream. I had him in my bed and he encompassed everything important to me at that moment.

I woke up to him whispering my name. I darted up immediately and was reminded that I was ill. I flew out of my room and to the bathroom, where I threw up nothing. Again. Thank fuck. I didn't want vomit all over my hair or my mouth while Teagan was there. Jesus, what the hell was he still doing there anyway? I could clearly see through the skylight of the bathroom that it was pitch black outside. How long had I been asleep? Why didn't anyone wake me up before then?

I went back into my bedroom to see Teagan was under my covers and his pants were on the floor. I looked at him, stunned. Sure, I had guys sneak into my room on occasion but never had a guy blatantly spent the night. My parents had to know he was still there since my car hadn't moved from the spot I parked in that afternoon.

He looked up to me with a concerned look on his face. "Are you feeling okay, Lizzie? You're really worrying me."

"I'm fine but it's really late, Teag. You have to go home. My parents are very traditional. They don't know that I spend all of my time at your house. They don't ask because I am old enough to do what I want but when it comes to their place, well…no sleepovers with guys until after marriage," I said, rolling my eyes.

He laughed. "My parents are stricter than that. I can't even kiss a girl on the couch in my parents' house. But your parents know I'm here, Lizzie. I talked to them when you went to sleep. They know you're sick. They know I'm not going to take advantage of you in your state," he said as he flung his arm out to scan my body. "Come here and let me hold you."

I crawled back into bed. "Why did you wake me up, then? I thought I heard you say my name."

He was quiet for a moment. His body tensed but I was too tired to look at him. I just waited for him to answer. He sighed and pulled me closer. "I'm glad to be here with you. It's nice to sleep in a bed on a frame."

"Why does it seem like you wanted to tell me something else? You paused for a long while and yet you told me something I already knew." I laughed.

"I'll take a cab to the train station in the morning but I really wanted to stay with you tonight," Teagan said, nuzzling into my neck.

"Don't waste your money on a cab. I'll drive you," I said, enjoying his face so close to mine.

"No, you're sick."

"I'm sure I'll be better by morning. I want to drive you to work."

"We'll see how you're feeling in the morning."

"Sure," I said as I nodded into my pillow, not giving a fucking shit about anything but his hands over my side and my lavender scented pillow.

"Good, now let's get some sleep. I set your alarm clock," he murmured. I could feel his heart beating really fast and I knew he wanted to tell me something important. Was he going to ask if we could have more after this summer fling? It seemed like he was getting a little more attached than just a tryst.

"Hmmm…" He chuckled and pulled me closer.

All thoughts of Monday morning's confusion on whether or not he still wanted to be near me were lost. He was worried about me after only two days and now he was there with me in my bed, snuggling up to my hair, and falling asleep with me in his arms. I felt the weight of that morning lift, and I cursed myself at over thinking our relationship. Teagan wasn't an asshole that just turned on a dime. He genuinely cared for me and wanted to be near me as much as I wanted to be near him. Knowing he wanted to be with me even when we weren't drinking and having sex was sobering. Instead, we were sharing an intimacy that far surpassed any physical attraction. We were lovers, sure. But in reality, I knew we were so much more.

Twenty-One

Dirty

The next morning, Teagan woke me up with a kiss to my forehead. When I opened my eyes, he was already freshly showered and dressed in his work clothes. I got up and threw my legs over the bed.

"You're ready?" I asked, squinting up to him with one eye.

"Yes, baby. I have to get to town. I packed you a bag. Come to the apartment and sleep there. Do you still have your key?" he asked.

"Yep. I'm really tired. I guess I could head over there, if it's okay with you," I said. Just thinking about all that driving was giving me a ridiculous headache.

He touched the back of his knuckles to my cheek. "I worry about my American girl. Come stay with me. It's the last night until I get back from New York on Monday."

I smiled over to him as I started throwing new clothes on. I didn't care that I hadn't showered in two days. I could take a shower at his place. He didn't seem to mind my scent all night, since every time I awoke, his arms were clamped around me. I grabbed my bag, my purse, and my keys and we headed down the stairs. Mom was sitting in the foyer, reading a magazine, and looked up. Her smile was bright and I gave her a cursory morning nod.

"Morning," Teagan said. "I'm stealing Lizzie away for the night. I promise that she's in good hands and I'll make sure she feels better."

"That's okay, Teag. You don't have to take care of me. I don't feel sick anymore. Mom, I'll call you later. It looks like the flu is gone."

"Oh, Lizzie. That's so great. I'll head out for work today, after all. Call the office if you need anything," she said as she gave both Teagan and me a hug.

After dropping Teagan off at his building downtown, I took Commonwealth up to his apartment. The streets were busy and I had to stop at every red light. Business people and tourists crossed the streets, never looking up from their maps or newspapers. I sighed at the blatant pedestrian-ruled city. Everyone was a shithead there when it came to getting on their way.

I pulled up to the side of the road and walked across the street, not caring if cars were coming. As I hit the sidewalk, I laughed that I, too, was a shithead.

I unlocked the door with my key, and both a familiar and disgusting scent had me stepping back into the hallway of Teagan's apartment building. Eww. I hadn't been there in days, so obviously no one was cleaning up after themselves. I always did the dishes and scrubbing to get beer and cigarette burns out of the carpet. I washed the bathroom every chance I could. But their place was a fucking disaster, and I could hardly breathe in through my nose. I noticed a ton of dishes piled in the sink and throughout the kitchen. At least four cases of empty beer bottles were strewn around the living room, and disgusting hurling equipment and clothes were laid out over every piece of furniture. You could literally see the clothing trail from Freddie's room to the bathroom, dirty underwear and all. I immediately felt gross. How had I stayed in that apartment all those weeks? Did I ever notice how God damn disgusting the place was?

I went to the kitchen and called Teagan's phone at work.

"Teagan Gallagher," he answered in a tired Irish accent.

"Hey, Teag. It's me. I'm here at your place, and this fucking hole is probably the most disgusting place I've ever seen." I scowled.

He chuckled under his breath. "Well, you sound back to your normal self again. We haven't had a girl around in a few days, so I guess you're probably spot on."

I scoffed at him loudly. "Did you make me come here to pick up after your filthy Irish arses?" I asked with the most terrible accent I could muster. I was better at it when I was drunk or pissed, as the guys called it.

"No, no, baby. I didn't know it was that dreadful. I'm sorry. I'll make the guys pick up their shit when we get home from work," he said, still laughing.

"Yeah, that's in like nine hours, Teag. I can't be here. It's tough to breathe without vomiting all over your dirty underwear."

His voice became sober. "Lizzie, don't leave. I only have tonight with you before I head out. Just stay or go walk in the park. Go buy yourself something. I have some bills in the front pocket of my jeans near my bed. Just don't leave," he pleaded.

"Umm. I guess I can head over to the bookstore for a while, but sincerely, this place is a wreck. You guys did a number on it while I was gone," I said with a frown, scanning the area of his room.

"Thank fuck," he said. "I really want to be with you tonight, okay?" he asked.

"Okay, Teag. Anything for my Irish boy," I said with a smile.

We hung up a few minutes later after talking about the meetings he had that day and how he would be away from his phone. After I stepped back from the receiver, the phone rang and I smiled.

"Do you miss me already?" I asked.

After a brief silence, an Irish female voice came over the receiver. "Hello, I'm calling for Teagan?" the girl inquired.

"Oh. I'm sorry about that. I thought you were someone else. No, no. He's at work," I said. "Can I give him a message?"

There was another long pause.

"No, that's okay. I'll ring him later," she said and hung up. Sister? Friend? Certainly Irish.

I went to Teagan's room to pull out the cash from his pocket and found a letter stuffed in an envelope with his name and address written on it. I gazed at it a bit, and while my curiosity was immense, I stuffed it back into his pants before my eyes landed on the drool on his pillow. Something inside me went to fucking hell and I threw myself towards the bathroom and started to throw up the cup of coffee I had that morning. I heaved and heaved until I finally could get up and wash my face. This place was an outlet for germs, and hell if I was going to be there, sucking in more flu. That place was probably what got me sick in the first place.

I grabbed my keys and bag and left. I didn't call Teagan, knowing he would talk me out of leaving. I drove myself home and went up to my neat, pristine room and played my guitar for the remainder of the afternoon.

After several successful sessions of playing, I went downstairs. No one was there so I went to the couch and lay there, listening to a thunderstorm looming in the distance. I sat there, staring at nothing at all. I felt completely vacant. Teagan and I were on a path to nowhere and I knew it. The more I fostered the connection, and the more interest he gave to me, the more I knew I wouldn't be able to let him go. He was my life that summer and nothing else mattered, especially me. Every waking moment, I thought about the night we met, the night we first had sex, the night he was possessive over me with Freddie. But first and foremost, I thought about his proclamation that he was my boyfriend to my oldest and dearest friends. I crawled on the leather couch and lay there, listening to the foreboding thunder and rain before I fell back asleep.

I awoke sometime later to Conner shaking me. "Hey, Lizzie, wake up. Teagan is on the phone. I told him you were sleeping but the guy doesn't give up. He said something about a letter and you not being at his place. He must have called like fifty freaking' times. Dude, this guy seriously has it bad for you," he said, holding the phone up to me.

I smiled. "The feeling's mutual," I whispered before I took the phone from his hands.

"Hello?" I said in a weak voice.

"Lizzie! How are you? Where are you?" he asked.

I laughed. "You called me, remember? I'm home. I got sick again at your place and just had to get out of there."

"Why didn't you leave a note or something?" He sounded really frustrated and I felt bad for him. There was nothing I could say. I got the hell out of there and I'm not even sure I locked the door when I left. Fuck.

"I don't know." I sighed. "I'm not really up to party tonight. I'm going to watch a few movies and hang here with my brother," I said as I looked at Conner with a bowl of popcorn on his lap, flipping through the pay per view list.

There was a long pause. "Well, then, I guess I'll see you next week when I return," he said firmly.

"Okay. Seriously, have a great time, and by the time you get back, I'll be all yours until you leave." I laughed.

"Sounds good, Lizzie O'Malley," he said with a smile.

"Oh, and Teag, before I forget, some girl, an Irish girl, called you while I was at your place earlier. She said she would call you later. Just to let you know."

There was yet another pause. Pausing on the phone is so frustrating. It was the worst thing to have a conversation with the dead end of the line.

He finally said, "Yeah, okay. It must have been my sister. I'll try to ring my house before I leave tomorrow night. Our flight is at eight, by the way, so I won't be able to call you tomorrow. We're going to pack and head for the airport right after work," he said.

"Okay, well, have fun," I said.

"Get better, baby. I'll miss you," Teagan said.

Twenty-Two

Bared

Friday morning, I woke up bright and early, ready to head out to my second summer session English Composition class. I had to submit a term paper and I was really confident I had done a good job on a personal memoir of music and how songs transported me back to certain times.

I heard my mother downstairs, making a lot of noise in the kitchen. As I rounded the marble breakfast nook, I was excited to see she had the waffle maker out and a huge pile on the table.

"Yummy," I said as I gave her a side hug and a kiss on the cheek.

"Do you feel like eating?" she asked brightly.

"Oh yeah, these look delicious, Mom. I can only eat for a few minutes. I have a term paper to run into school," I said in a rush, spreading butter and syrup on the waffles.

She grinned at me with the most pride I'd seen in years.

I smiled back and started on my waffles. Teagan came to mind and I thought about how certain songs already reminded me of him. "Round Here," by Counting Crows and pretty much anything by David Gray. I shrugged my shoulders to push the thought of Teagan out of my head for what seemed like the hundredth time in the forty-five minutes I'd been awake.

After the fourth bite, my mouth started to salivate and I became breathless, like I was going to have a panic attack. My mom looked at me, and as she started to say something, I ran to the downstairs bathroom and threw every little piece of waffle up.

"That's it!" she said in a scream that made me wince. "You've been sicker much longer than Conner was. You're going to see Dr. Collins today." She started to fumble around with her address book.

"Okay." That was all I could say. I was so sick of being sick. It was never ending, and I was malnourished and weak. I felt great the day before and that morning, but maybe I just ate the waffles too fast.

I could hear my mother making an appointment for me on the phone, and while I was washing my face, she yelled through the door. "I have an appointment for you at one, right after the doctor gets back from lunch. There won't be any wait. Can you get to school and get to the appointment on time?"

"Yes, Mom. Thank you," I muttered.

Dropping off my paper to my professor and telling her I had a doctor's appointment was refreshing because of all the lame excuses I had come up with when I was too damn hung over to make it to class, this one was actually true.

When I got to Dr. Collins' office, the rain was starting to come in again and I pulled on my black trench coat. It wasn't waterproof, but I felt like it shielded me to some degree. I signed in with the receptionist and she made it a point for me to say hello to my mother. Jesus, this was such a small town. But a small town in a big city wasn't always so bad. I felt comforted knowing my mother had set up the appointment, and I was going to finally get some medicine to feel better.

As the doctor's assistant took my blood pressure, temperature, and weight, she reassured me everything looked normal and told me to go into the first room on the right. I asked her if I should disrobe and she shook her head.

"This is just a flu consultation, honey." She smiled.

A few moments later, Dr. Collins came in and gave me a warm smile.

As I shook his hand, he looked me over and said, "Lizzie, you've grown into such a nice young woman. I know I've been around a long time since I remember when you had teeth missing and pigtails."

I laughed and returned his warm smile.

"So, what seems to be going on?" he asked.

"Well, I've had the flu now for more days than my mother finds necessary. I throw up, sleep a lot, and have occasional diarrhea," I said, barely self-conscious about being completely honest with my doctor.

"Well, you don't have a temperature, so no infection." He looked down at the chart.

He whipped his head up and gave me a look that I couldn't comprehend.

"Lizzie, are you sexually active?" he asked in a quiet voice.

I could immediately feel my face warm. Never in my dreams did I imagine Dr. Collins asking me about sex. He was my freaking pediatrician, for fuck's sake. I had an OBGYN, so was this really his business?

"Lizzie?" he asked.

I smiled and he nodded.

"I'm going to have one of the nurses come in and explain how to use our pregnancy tests. Just lay back a minute and I'll have her come in. It is improbable, as I am sure you're careful, but it's just a start so we can figure out what might really be going on."

He headed out the door and my heart started to race. Pregnancy test? What a laugh. There was no way I was pregnant. Teagan and I had been completely careful, and when the condom did break, I made sure to count my ovulation dates to confirm I was way out of that window of possibility. I must have gone over that in my head ad nauseam because I can still rattle off that the 19th through the 23rd were my fertile times.

A nurse came back in with a cup and showed me to the bathroom, instructing me to pee in the cup. I nodded, feeling so stupid for giving any thought at all to being pregnant. I returned the cup to the stainless steel shelf in the bathroom and headed back to the room I was assigned.

After a half an hour, I was in full panic mode. No one had returned to the room. No one came to take my temperature. I was pacing the room and I knew I was leaving marks in the tiled floor. I stilled when I heard a light knock. Dr. Collins came in with the nurse that had given me the cup.

He patted the chair next to him and looked at me with a smile.

"Elizabeth, you don't have the flu, honey. You're going to have a baby," he said.

I shot straight off my chair and started breathing so hard, the nurse raced over to start rubbing my back.

"No. I'm not. We've been safe. We…"

"Lizzie, we did two separate tests and you're pregnant. Do you know when it could have happened?"

I stuttered out something incomprehensible and shook my head.

"Lizzie, I would like to do an exam to see how large your fetus is. That will give us some timeline of how far along you are," he said. "Put on this gown and leave it open in the back. Both of us will be back when you're ready."

I started shaking. Thoughts and words could not even come close to leaving my chattering teeth. All at once, I felt hot and extremely cold, and I swayed back and forth for several minutes. I stood with the gown in my hands and stared at the blank white wall of the doctor's office then I started to cry. I couldn't be pregnant. I couldn't get pregnant. I didn't get pregnant. I was not pregnant. There was a light knock on the door and I immediately jumped. I had no idea how long I had been standing there, fully clothed, but I immediately yelled out, "NO!" I didn't know exactly what I was saying no to. The doctor coming in, the doctor not coming in, me being pregnant, me not being pregnant. In that instance, nothing made any sense whatsoever.

I opened the door and flew past the nurse and the doctor. They looked dumbstruck and I shook my head all the way down the hall, past the reception area, and out into the humid downpour in my hometown. I stood outside my car, my hands trembling to find my keys. They dropped into a muddy puddle and I sank down against the car, my whole body encompassed by the water. I couldn't feel wet. I couldn't feel the car. I couldn't feel the blood that ran from my palms as my nails bit into them. A car drove by while another was trying to back out of the parking lot and a loud horn brought me out of my trance. I grabbed the keys from the water, stood up, and plunged into the car. Holding the steering wheel, I had no idea where to go.

If I went home like that, my mother would know, and she absolutely could never know. If I went to Teagan's work like that, I, well, I really didn't know what to do or say. If I went to a restaurant, I couldn't eat, and for fuck's sake, I was going to be sick again. I opened the car door and heaved.

The car ride to Teagan's didn't take long enough. I knew he wasn't there. I knew I wasn't going into the apartment that would forever change my life. But something inside me felt the need for him to call me baby, for him to cuddle against me, for him to call me his American girl. Maybe then, I would be able to take a deep breath.

When I parked at Teagan's apartment, the rain was coming down so hard that the instant I stepped out, my fully clothed body felt like I was standing in a steamy shower. I walked down Commonwealth Avenue in a trance, not caring what people thought or the huge splashes of water that cars sprayed over my body. I shook but I wasn't cold. I was shocked. Shocked into a complete oblivion that I'd never felt before and the knot in my stomach about having to say the two words to anyone made me even more rigid as I took in the view of the wet sidewalk.

I looked down at my watch and saw that it was four. If I didn't catch Teagan before he left for his flight, I wouldn't get a hug or a word from him for three days, and I didn't know where I would be in three days. I wanted to be numb. Number.

I pivoted and started back up Commonwealth to Teagan's apartment. As I started to become aware again, my whole body shook in anticipation of what he might say. It made me walk faster. Would he want this baby? Would I move to Ireland? Could we be parents together? I was more than "in like" with him and I knew he felt the same way so would this change anything? When I got to his stairs, I sat down and let the rain pour down on me as I thought of the alternate answer he would give me. Get rid of it. That's what made the most sense. He would tell me to get rid of it.

The T came to a stop at Cleveland Circle and I looked up to see some of the guys running to the apartment to get out of the downpour. I knew when Teagan's eyes finally landed on me and I quickly stood up to meet him. He was standing across the street, pivoting his eyes from the oncoming traffic to where I was. He looked perplexed but calm. I cringed and waited.

The other guys breezed past me, muttering shit about me being crazy for sitting out in the rain and asking what happened to my key. I smiled at them and nodded. Teagan came to a full stop in front of me. Beads of rain poured down his head, into his shirt, and onto his pants. His shoes were already drenched.

"Come inside, Lizzie. You're all wet. God, you're fucking soaked through. What the hell happened?" he asked.

"I...I just came here to tell you something then I'll leave," I said, shaking uncontrollably.

"Jesus, Lizzie. You have to come inside." He pulled me up from underneath my arms. He pressed my body to his as he fished out his keys and unlocked the door then pushed through the slightly opened door to the apartment. I immediately noticed how clean it was and smiled on the inside, thankful that I had a distraction from myself for an instant.

"It… It… looks really… good in here," I said, still chattering.

Teagan pulled me into his room. Cian was packing a duffel bag and he turned around to see us. When he actually looked at me, he cleared his throat and said, "I have a phone call to make."

Teagan locked the door behind him and immediately started to strip me of my clothes. I furiously shook my head as I tightened my arms around my trench coat. I didn't want him to touch me before he knew what I knew. I was dripping rain into his carpet but I didn't care.

He closed his eyes in frustration, and when he opened them, he gave me a firm look.

I whispered, hardly audible to my own ears. "Teagan, I'm pregnant."

Twenty-Three

Defeated

I took a step back from Teagan and leaned on the wall, sliding down to the floor. I looked at him through my wet hair and watched him struggle with several different emotions. Shock was the most apparent on his face. Then he scrubbed his hand through his hair and down the back of his neck. He repeated this over and over again. Finally, after what felt like forever in silence, he got down on his knees in front of me and kissed my forehead.

"Lizzie, I have to go talk to Cian. I'm not leaving you right now. I can't go away. I won't leave now. I can't..." he rambled.

"No, you don't have to stay. I'll still be here when you get home. One of us might as well have a good weekend."

"I'm not leaving."

"Teag..."

"Enough. I'm staying. No more discussion," he said with finality.

I looked up to him and just whispered, "Okay." No New York City. No Statue of Liberty. No American dream. This was the most monumental American girl disaster.

Teagan left the room and all the wetness from my body finally shocked me enough that I began to remove all my clothing. By the time I was taking my underwear off, I was sobbing and throwing all my wet items against the walls. I went into the walk-in closet, closed the door, and crumbled in a fetal position in the corner.

The walk-in closet became my respite from the outside world for the following hours. Teagan came in and sat with me, not saying anything other than he was not leaving. He hadn't undressed and he hadn't moved from my side. His hand finally lifted and he put it on top of mine. He didn't look at me and I didn't look at him. We just sat there silently.

"Teagan," I whispered.

He glanced at me like he didn't even realize I was there. He looked pained and pale. His face was drawn down and I didn't know what to say. What was I supposed to say? Hey, I'm going to have your fucking baby but you're leaving next month forever. Have a nice fucking trip.

"Teagan, I went to the doctor because of the flu. It…it wasn't the flu."

"Lizzie, I'm certain you're telling me the truth. For fuck's sake, you were soaking wet when I found you. You can't stop shaking. Tonight, let's just take it easy. We need to eat something and you should take a hot shower," he said rigidly. "We can talk this weekend."

"Okay," I said, pretending not to hear the detachment in his voice.

After picking at my take out chicken parmesan, I looked up to see Teagan sitting across from me at the dinner table. It hit me that he and I never sat there to have dinner, and the automatic sense of foreboding made me feel small. The scene was so domestic. He didn't want me tucked away in his room to feed each other, like we had so many times before. He didn't want to put on music and sit on the couch while we gorged on food. He actually sat me in the chair and pulled the aluminum away from

my steaming meal then took his seat across from me, never
saying a word.

When he looked up at me, he smiled but it never hit his
eyes. I darted my eyes back down at my meal and shook off the
feeling that I was ruined. I was broken. I had a baby, his baby,
inside of me and I couldn't feel comfort. I couldn't feel anything
but hollow. Hollow like a pitch black corridor leading to nowhere
and never ending.

He pulled our meals away and sat right next to me. He
brushed the now dried hair from my eyes and made a small,
unintelligible sound, something between a moan and a cry. My
eyes shot up to him.

"I'm not sure how you feel right now. I wish I did. I wish
I could know," he said.

"No, Teagan, you don't know how I fucking feel. Do you
think I've ever been pregnant before? Do you think I've ever
waited so long for one person to give me one fucking word of
comfort? You're so quiet. You won't even look at me, and when
you do, it's fucking fake. You pity me. You wreck me with the
silence. You fucking wrecked me. I wrecked me. I never should
have…" He broke off my rage with a firm, passionate kiss. He
pressed his hands on my shoulders like he wanted me to stay
planted where I was forever. He kissed me deep and solid like
only one other time I could remember. I broke the kiss and my
trembling hand went to my mouth. I could feel the burn, the
understanding, the final fucking epiphany.

"You remember when the condom broke," I asked.

He nodded.

"But I keep thinking that's impossible. I am so regular and I know my cycle. It broke only a couple weeks ago. I counted my fertile times. We weren't even in the proximity. I cleaned everything out of me that night. I willed it away and you... You... told me everything would be okay," I said with a pounding heart that I knew he could feel radiate between us.

He nodded again.

I shot out of my chair and headed to his bedroom to collect my things. All the things I had ever left there. I not only ruined myself, my future, but I ruined him. What kind of girl did he think I was? I was a knocked up American slut and I had no business being in that foreign place. That place meant nothing anymore. It was a trap of lies and deceit. It was a trap and I could feel the tightness in my chest before I started to sob once more. I never cried so hard or so loud, wailing out to the world that I needed relief. I needed something. New hope. Some kind of promise that I was a good person. I was a good person.

I looked up to see Teagan leaning against the doorjamb. His hands were in the pockets of his khaki cargo shorts and he looked at me with reverence.

"You're not going anywhere. You always flee. You always leave. We're not even close to talking, and already, you want to run away," he said.

"Yes," I whispered through my now silent sobs, hiccupping on the breath caught in my throat.

He came in the room, slammed the door, and yelled, "Fuck that, Lizzie. Not this fucking time. You stay here with me. You stay until we decide what to do. You stay until there are no more words to say. You are not the only one in this and I will not let you carry this burden on your shoulders. Not this time. You've had plenty of them in the past and this time, we'll not leave this room until we both decide what to do."

I was scared. I had never heard anyone, other than my father when I was repeatedly grounded in high school, ever talk to me that way.

"Bastard," I said.

He crooked up a smile and came to close the distance between us.

"I care about you," he said as he laid his hand on my stomach. "This is a lot to take in and decisions need to be made. Not now. But soon."

He grabbed me in a hug and we sank onto the bed. He lay over me, kissing my eyes that still held pools of tears. He kissed my mouth, he kissed my neck, and as he slowly started to lift my shirt, I realized that he was taking the most care, gentle and light, to make love to me. I lost myself in his intimate touch, his need to be inside me. Every caught breath between us, every gasp, assured me I wasn't a bad person. I was a decent person who made a mistake. And he was, too. We moved together, skin on skin, for the first time all summer, while he looked into my eyes with a promise that everything would be okay, even if it was only in that moment.

My vulnerability and his strength balanced into a passion that grew more and more intense. When he finally came inside me, all I could feel was relieved. I was comforted but still so hollow. No matter how many times we made love, it would never be enough to fill the emptiness in my soul.

Teagan cuddled up behind me, and after kissing my sweaty brow, he whispered, "I'm so sorry, Lizzie."

We never slept that night. The pounding of our hearts and the rain pelting against the window kept us wide awake. The storm was between us.

Twenty-Four

Morals and Traditions

I must have fallen asleep after the sun came up because I don't remember watching it through the window. It wasn't raining anymore, and Teagan wasn't in the bed with me. I propped up on my elbows to see him sitting on Cian's bed, clothed and looking perfect. Delicious. Then, I remembered why I was there and why he had his head down in his hands.

"Teag?" I asked.

His head came up wearily, and his eyes were bloodshot and empty. He looked like he didn't get any sleep at all. His hands started to move over the rough stubble on his face and he wouldn't look at me.

I knew I had my answer to what was to come.

"Liz, I've thought and thought about this all night," he started. "Jesus, my mother just called not an hour ago to ask how I was doing. She thinks I'm working and doing the right thing here. Do you know how hard it is to not to be able to tell her that I got a girl pregnant?"

"I'm sorry." I said in anger. "You're worried about what your mother is going to think about you knocking someone up? Can you be anymore insensitive about this? I just found out yesterday afternoon. My own family doesn't even know. I came right to you," I said, flailing my arm towards him across the room.

"Okay, so we're both freaking out," he said calmly.

"Ya think?" I asked.

We stayed like that, just staring at each other for several minutes. I got up and put on my shirt and underwear and immediately felt the nausea. I bolted out the door to the bathroom. I closed and locked the door before I threw up what looked like the chicken parmesan I had the night before. A gentle knock came to the door and I stayed silent. Besides my intermittent vomiting, I sat there next to the toilet and said nothing. I looked at my toes, totally dazed. Freaking out wasn't even close to what I was feeling. Teagan could kick me out and ask me never to come back. I could leave and never come back. But the insistent knocking made me believe that he wouldn't leave me alone until this situation was completely resolved. I didn't move from the floor until well after I was done throwing up. When I turned on the water, the knocking came louder and Teagan's voice came through.

"Lizzie. You can't hide in there. We need to talk. We need to talk until we can't talk anymore. I'm sorry I freaked out. I just didn't want to talk to my mother this morning, of all mornings. Please come out and let's do this, okay?" he pleaded.

I unlocked the door and he immediately opened it, grabbing me in a hug and taking me back down to his room. He closed the door and we sat on his bed at the same time. We both started talking at once then immediately stopped. I nodded towards him and he began the speech that will forever haunt my dreams, my fears, my soul, my heart and my life.

"My mom and dad grew up in a very traditional catholic Irish family. The value of marriage and children is very important to my family. They don't know that I've even had sex," he said.

I snorted and looked at him, thinking he was joking. He was certainly not.

"So, when you find an Irish girl, you date her then you ask for her father's blessing before you marry her. Before you have children."

I quietly sat there, feeling like I was suddenly transported back into a Jane Austen book and I was the stupid whore. Which sister was I in Pride and Prejudice? Why was I even thinking about books? I didn't want to feel the denial. I wanted to feel a part of something that I could relate to but I couldn't. The whole situation was so foreign to me. I was a colossal mistake and we both knew it at that moment. But fucking all hell, I was in love with Teagan. It was so crystal clear to me then. I went to him and hugged him with reverence and the tears started to stream down my face. It was all a waste. I started to hyperventilate. I tried to stop the sobs. I didn't know this me. I didn't know how to fix it. I wanted to punch him and I wanted to kiss him, to make him love me back. I wanted him to give up everything to be with me. I wanted him forever. My sobs wouldn't stop. I tried so hard not to let anyone see the raw in me, but now that I did, it didn't make any difference. He held me back at arm's length.

"I know I did this with you, to you. We made a baby. I understand the depth of this. You are pregnant and I'm the father but Lizzie, I'm not staying in America. I'm not going to be here if you want to keep the baby. I'm not going to know the child, and my family will never know that you and the baby exist," he said with sadness. He started to tear up and I began to sway my head back and forth. The harsh words of complete rejection did me in. Something died in that moment. Shot in the heart, stomped on, drowned, bludgeoned, ripped away, exploded, and imploded. I had nothing left.

"Do you want me to get an abortion?" I asked.

He shook his head slowly. "I want the choice to be yours. I can't be a part of your decision but I will be there if you do decide to have an abortion. If you don't, then I can't be a part of this. Ever," he said. He knew that the words were blunt. I could see it in his face. I was never his. If I had been, he would welcome a part of both of us.

"I knew I never belonged to you," I said as I started to wring my hands together.

Teagan didn't want to purposely hurt me but he did, nonetheless. He couldn't be a father because it wasn't in the Irish traditional way. He couldn't date me, meet my father, ask for my hand in marriage or have babies with me because I was American. I never knew him. Never like that. David Gray's song rang in my head, *"Say hello, wave goodbye."*

We both remained silent. I felt the weight of loneliness. It was all on me and the burden of it was unbearable. My choice. Pro-choice. Pro-Life. I didn't have a job, I lived with my parents, I drank like a fish, and the man I believed I was in love with and the father of the person growing inside me just dismissed me. Dismissed.

The phone rang and Teagan went to answer it. He came back a minute later and held it out to me.

"It's your mum," he said blankly.

I took it gingerly from his hands.

"Hi, Mom," I said with a quiver in my voice.

"Elizabeth. How did the doctor's appointment go? Is everything alright? Conner went through the caller ID and I didn't know where you went to last night. I've been worried," she said in a rush.

"I'm fine. The doctor just said it was the flu and everyone was getting it." I looked pointedly at Teagan as I answered her.

"Oh, good," she said.

"Mom, we're heading out to the park for Teagan's hurling match. Talk later, okay?"

"Sure, come home soon."

We said our goodbyes and I let the phone fall to the floor. I just lied to my mother and that felt like a knife through the remainder of the heart I had left. I started to sob again and Teagan came towards me. I held up my hands and he backed off.

"Don't. Touch. Me," I said.

I knew if he touched me, I would beg, and I was not going to beg for his love. I would never, ever beg another man to love me. First, it was Chase, and now the father of my child. If he's putting this decision in my hands alone, then he doesn't want me. He doesn't want a future with me. That was never in question. I finally knew that all along, he didn't want to say he loved me. He didn't want me to go to Ireland. I wasn't his American girl. I was absolutely nothing. I was his American burden.

Teagan and I spent the day together as two mindless zombies wandering the world in search of something to fill the ache. We didn't hold hands or laugh at anything. We wandered around downtown Boston on a Saturday, taking in the tourists and their zoom lenses. At one point, he put his hand on the small of my back to lead me underground to the T, but it felt as if he had burned me. I knew it was standard for him to touch me

184

because our hands were always all over each other no matter where we were, but I felt like everything he told me that morning scathed my soul. He knew I withdrew from him the minute I warned him off from trying to hug me. I needed to accept that he was already the ghost standing next to me, the transparent being not talking to me any longer, and the past shadow that drew me into the deep, darkest thoughts of devastation.

We headed back to his apartment in silence, and I sat down on his bed. He put his hand on my leg and put his head on my shoulder. I made no move and I couldn't. I was all alone. He tried to comfort me but inside I was full of grief and guilt. I couldn't blame anyone but myself. I had my eyes wide open going into this and his aloofness was palpable.

"Do you want to spend the night with me again?" Teagan asked.

I stared at his closed door and because I didn't know where else to go or who else to be, I nodded. I was in way too deep. I was cut in so many places that I felt like I was bleeding out from every part of my body. Being outside and watching people live their normal lives took me out of my head, but the minute I stepped back into the apartment, I was muted inside. No words, no actions, no me. I had a mantra running through my head the entire day. I was pro-choice. I was pro-choice.

I was pro-choice. I'd always believed a woman had the right to choose, but at that moment, my political standings didn't make me feel empowered or any closer to an action. I wanted, no needed, someone else to choose for me. I didn't know what the hell I was going to do and Teagan sure as fuck made it clear that he wasn't going to be anything of influential substance.

"Lizzie, talk to me," Teagan said.

I looked up to see that he was right next to me, inching his body close, so intimately.

"I'm not sure what to say. I found out that I am pregnant twenty-four hours ago and within twelve of those hours, you told me you wouldn't be in the life of the baby you made with me because of the traditions in your family," I said.

He started to say something but I stopped him.

"You talk about traditions but all that runs through my head is morals. Where are your morals? In my very conservative family, we don't take pregnancy lightly. Yes, I'm pro-choice but not in the form of using it as birth control. I would never wish this decision on anyone and I doubt any other woman would, either. But you...you're forcing me to change the course of my life, by either raising a child on my own or killing it," I said, a tear coming down my face.

"Did you ever think about what my family will think of this?" I asked, placing a palm over my chest. "You were so determined to have a summer of fun. Is this fucking fun for you? And yes, before you answer that, I agreed to this... this...whatever it is. But this is all sorts of fucked up now. This is serious, life-altering decision making and I can't believe that you would just expect me to not have deep and dark thoughts about my body, my mind, my family, myself," I said.

Teagan sighed and pulled me into his arms.

"I got scared earlier after I talked to my mom, and I guess I just reacted. I didn't take into account how your life would be changed. It's just that my life is in Cork. I can't stay here. I don't have a visa. I have to finish school. It's what is expected of me, and if I make this your choice, then it's all I can do. I can't tell you to have the baby, knowing what I have to do. I can't tell you to have an abortion or give it up for adoption because I don't know how you feel on those types of issues."

I sat up from him immediately. "You don't give one shit about me, do you?" I asked.

"Jesus, Lizzie, I care very much for you. You've been so amazing but give me a break here. We were as safe as we could be and I never wanted to intentionally get you pregnant then hurt you. That was never my intention. Out of everything else you hear me tell you, you have to understand that. I care about what you choose to do because I care about you. It's just... I can't put it into words. I guess I just can't be what you think you want me to be. I never was," he solemnly said.

I nodded my head slowly and said, "No, you won't ever be what I wanted you to be but not because of what happened before yesterday. It's because now that I'm up shit creek, you've bailed on me. I guess I can only blame myself for expecting something from someone who claims to care about me."

We sat there in silence for hours. The night sky was lighter than the dark room we sat in. Neither of us even shifted on the bed. We were permanent fixtures in the room, and the more silence there was, the easier I could relax and clear my mind. I wasn't afraid anymore. I was numb but not scared and I didn't feel reckless. I looked at him and his withdrawn and desolate face looked back to me.

"I can't have a baby," I said. It was true. If I couldn't get my life straightened out on my own, my baby would never come first. Although my life was unconventional, I would have a baby the traditional way. I would go to college, get married, and then

187

have children. I would not have a child with a man I'd never see again. I would never even know how to explain that to my child.

He looked back at me and firmly said, "Okay. I'll help you. Set up the appointment and I'll take care of the costs and I'll be there for you, whatever you need."

I finally exhaled the breath I had been holding for hours. My decision was made and we both seemed to relax back into what felt like normalcy again. He went out to the kitchen and came back with sandwiches and beer. We sat and ate tentatively. We were quiet. We slowly inched towards one another and cuddled on the bed. We didn't ever talk about the future of the pregnancy again.

Twenty-Five

There Is No Place, Especially Home

Teagan and I spent the remainder of the weekend under lock and key in his bedroom, only leaving the bubble we put ourselves in to answer the door for delivery food and to use the bathroom. His touches were soft and gentle. Occasionally, I caught him looking down at my bare stomach with a resigned look on his face. The sensation of my love and understanding of his gazes somehow made me fall more and more for him. If I kept this baby, he would always be a part of me. Never seeing Teagan again after a few more weeks made my heart bleed. The idea that his hands would never touch me in any way made me want to keep one thing of him inside, stretching the touch of him from outside my body. I was being so fucking ridiculous but I knew, after all, that I had fallen deeply in love with Teagan and the heartbreak of losing him overwhelmed every other feeling I had over this pregnancy.

Monday morning came in a flash. He started to dress for work as I lay there naked and sheetless on his bed. The soft love making the night before had confirmed all the feelings I had for him, and while I knew a huge shift in reality was only a few hours away, I could imagine what it would be like to stay in that bubble forever. Teagan reassured me all weekend that everything would turn out the way it was supposed to and I believed him. I trusted him, even if he didn't want to be in my future.

I shook the thoughts out of my head and started to dress. When I sat on the bed to pull my sandals on, he bent in front of me.

"Lizzie, this is all bad timing but I have a friend coming into town on Wednesday. It's been planned for a long time and I

189

don't want our situation to ruin their time here. I want you to go to your parents and explain everything, but then I want you to come back to me so I can be with you during this time. I want to know everything. But after Wednesday, I need some space through the weekend. It doesn't mean I don't care about you. It just means that I owe it to my friend to entertain them. I hope you can understand that," he said.

Thinking about how the next several days would go, I just nodded. I didn't care about his friends or partying. I had more important decisions to make before I could get back my life. Teagan was clearly lost to me already, and it was time to grow a spine and face my problems head on.

As I headed out the door with him, he held my hand, and before he took off for the T downtown, he gave me a slow, lingering kiss. It was a kiss of comfort, reassuring me that everything would work out.

Half an hour later, I parked in my driveway and sat there. I knew my mother was still inside but I couldn't remember if my dad was out of town. I knew Conner would still be asleep from his concert the previous night. As I walked up the stairs, the door flew open and my mother stood there with a stern look on her face.

"You never once called me to tell me where you were all weekend. I know you were with Teagan, but geez, Lizzie, it would have been nice to get a call. Are you feeling better?" She asked, her tone going from frustration to warmth. How she did that, I didn't know. It was a trademark Mom thing. Mom never stayed mad or upset for long.

"Mom, I'm old enough to do what I want. I'm not a teenager anymore," I said as I gave her a kiss on the cheek.

Something in the house smelled dreadful. Oh fuck, was that bacon? All of a sudden, my mind thought of pigs eating slop from a disgusting barrel and I flew past her to the bathroom to throw up bile. Mom came right up beside me and rubbed my back.

"Oh no, you still have the bug," she said.

I shook my head. As I lifted off the floor, flushed the toilet and threw water in my face, I caught the reflection of my mother in the mirror. She was clearly confused. Did she actually not know what morning sickness looked like? For God's sake.

I took her hand and led her into the sitting room, facing her on the floral sofa. My head turned down. I stuttered to find the words.

"Lizzie?" she asked.

I looked into her eyes, tears clouding my vision. "Mom, Teagan and I. Well, we made a horrible mistake. Not a mistake, it was an accident but Mom…"

She cut me off by standing abruptly. "Oh my God, Lizzie. You're pregnant. You're pregnant," she said accusingly.

I slowly nod once.

She came down to sit closer and took my hands into hers. Her eyes were filled with tears and she wiped them away hastily. "So, I'm going to be a grandmother?" she asked. Something flashed across her face. Hope, determination, happiness. Shit, I thought, drawing the word out into a three second drawl.

"Mom." I grasped her hands. "He doesn't want it. He doesn't see things the way you and Daddy do. He has to leave and his traditions far outweigh his morals in this situation. He's made it clear that it would never be possible for him to go through with this. And I… I… can't do this alone," I said with my head turned down, not meeting her gaze.

She tensed and took her hands out of mine like I had burned her.

"Lizzie, you cannot be thinking… We are not that type of family. Babies are a miracle and yes, the circumstances are troubling, but you can't possibly be thinking of terminating the pregnancy," she said with vehemence.

I looked her in the eyes and I answered her question with mine.

Just then, Conner came down the stairs, barreling toward us in a white tank top and his baby blue boxers. His red hair stood up every which way and I smiled at his way of making an appearance every time. Then I cringed.

His eyes locked on my mother's, who was clearly crying now without wiping any wetness away. Conner looked at my swollen eyes and sat down on the adjacent sofa.

"Oh my God," he said with a look of panic. "What happened? Who died?"

Then my mother started to tremble and sob.

Conner looked at me and I said, "No one died, Conner. But I need Dad here so I can explain. I have a problem and I need my family's support."

My mother stood up abruptly, ran up the stairs, and called my dad down from his home office. So he wasn't away this week. Great, just my luck. Facing the cavalry was the hardest damn thing I've ever done. I crossed my arms over my chest then crossed my legs as Conner studied me like he was trying to get the truth from my body language. I gave him a warm smile but he didn't return it. He was a momma's boy and no way was he going to let his mother cry without intervening.

Minutes passed before my mom and dad stepped into the room. Both sat on either side of Conner and I sat alone on the sofa. I was alone. Clearly, the physical boundary between us was a show of Mom's total objection to my decision.

I took a deep breath and spoke gently about how I met Teagan and how we were having fun this summer. I obviously left the obscene drinking out of the equation, but I'm sure that was assumed. I told them how we were careful but no protection is 100% guaranteed...and we were that .001 percent. Dad instantly registered where I was headed and put his head in his hands. Conner looked to me expectantly for the remainder of the story. I only spoke to him as I finished with the choice that I made and listed all the reasons I couldn't have the baby. No job, no father, no explanation in the long term, no baby.

Dad stood and went back upstairs. He did that when he had nothing nice to say. Conner looked pissed.

"Lizzie, what the fucking hell have you done? And this Teagan guy... What a fucking douche bag. He just wants to leave a girl that he knocked up and never think twice about it? He's a fucking mother fucker. Where in God's name does he live because I'm going to beat the living hell out of him." He started to pace in front of the fireplace. It was funny how Conner sort of made up for the lack of flames with his seething looks at me. Mom stayed quiet on the sofa and continued to weep softly. I started to cry at her disappointed eyes and Conner's furious tone as he rambled on about how much of a fuck up I was and how I should have known better about shitheads that only think with

193

their dicks. I shuttered at that thought, thinking back on all the times Teagan's dick wasn't anywhere near me, but his heart was.

Mom abruptly stood and looked at me with a pointed finger. "There is no way in hell you're going to get rid of the baby that's growing inside you. I don't care what your reasons are. I'll take care of my grandchild, if no one else will. That is what's going to happen, and if you don't accept that reality, then you're not welcome in this house," she said sternly then walked out of the room. Soon, I heard sobs coming from the kitchen.

Conner swore under his breath and followed his mother to the kitchen. I watched all my family walk out on me, giving me an ultimatum that I couldn't take. Every breath I took was ragged and forced. The clutch on my gut was fierce and unforgiving. My immediate reaction was, once again, there in a flash. There was no way I was going to ignore it this time. I ran up the stairs and locked my bedroom door. I grabbed a huge bag and started throwing clothes and accessories in it. It was a flurry of action in my urgency to get the fuck out of that house. That house was no longer my home. It was a place that didn't accept me. It wasn't the comforting safe haven that it once was, and I knew without a doubt, that even if I slept in my car, I didn't have any options. The father of my baby was indifferent, and my own parents were firm in their decision for my destiny. I was trapped, and as my ragged breathing became too much, I zipped up the bag and quietly slipped down the stairs, closing the door with quiet precision.

As I started the car, I looked back to the front porch where I locked eyes on Conner. The desolate look on his face was more than I could bear. I mouthed, "I'm sorry" at him and threw the clutch into reverse. I looked back in my rearview mirror and saw Conner on the steps with his head in his hands. I started to cry. When the trembling got to be too much, I pulled over three blocks away. I had nowhere to go. I wouldn't go back to Teagan's like this. He would be upset that my decision was now skewed by my family's firm pro-life stance. I couldn't go home because my family rejected my decision, and there was no way I could rip my body apart. I thought through the catalog of people I could go to and only one name came to mind. One person would listen to my story without judgment. He would only listen. He would always be there no matter the distance and the time. I would be able to hide. I would go unnoticed, a nameless face in the crowd.

Twenty-Six

Refuge

I stopped at a payphone before heading north on I-95 towards Newbury. It didn't take long to find his house. I'd never been there before, since he moved out of the city while I was in Oregon. When I got to the door with my large bag, Sean opened it before I could knock. He gave me a big grin until he saw my face, and then his look changed immediately to concern.

I took in his appearance. A white, old school Metallica tee and rough khaki pants reminded me how long it had been since we spent more than three hours together. As teenagers, we had secret sleepovers at his place. I would crawl through his window in the middle of the night and we'd smoke pot and listen to music. I would end up sleeping there, and even though we never had sex, he cuddled with me like we were an intimate couple. He took my bag and opened one arm for me to come in. He guided me past his roommate on the couch, whom I've never met, and directly into his bedroom. Bongs, clothes, and a large music system took up his room. Apart from the cream colored comforter, it was exactly what his room looked like when he lived only miles from me. I sighed and fell face up on his bed.

He put on the Pixies Doolittle album then lay next me. He grabbed the fingers of my hand and stared up at the ceiling. I felt so comforted just knowing that I didn't have to explain anything going on in my fucked up life. Sean would certainly listen and offer no judgment, but I was embarrassed that he actually met Teagan and I couldn't listen to another guy making him out to be a giant asshole. If he said anything, it would be that.

"Lizzie, I hate to see that you've been crying," he softly said. I almost didn't hear him.

"Sean, I've really fucked things up. I don't know what to do. I'm so scared and feel so ashamed of myself," I said.

"If I had a dollar for every time you said the words, I fucked up, I wouldn't have to work anymore," he said, nudging my shoulder with his.

"I know, I know. But this is monumental. Big. Probably the most fucked up situation I've ever been in. My family isn't speaking to me and I've lost a guy I think I've fallen in love with. No, I know I've fallen in love with," I said, looking sideways to him.

"That Irish dude?" he asked with a cocked eyebrow. "I was going to tell you. He just doesn't seem like your type. You normally go for the tall and dangerous bad boy types. He seemed too normal. Not your typical Lizzie guy."

"Chase wasn't tall."

"No, but he was an asshole to let you go, Lizzie. You aren't someone that I would ever take for granted," he said.

I turned over and started to cuddle into him. He was the sweetest male friend I'd ever had and I always thought it was too bad that we never had any chemistry together.

"Tell me," he said, kissing the top of my head.

I repeated the story for the second time that day, thinking I would be telling it for the rest of my life. Every moment of Teagan and my love making, the times we cherished at the wedding and that weekend of bliss. I touched my neck to feel his necklace and it no longer made me feel special. It felt like a slap in the face. I immediately took it off and tucked it into a side pocket of my bag. When I crawled back into Sean's arms, he asked me what I was going to do. I told him I was leaning towards abortion and he nodded his head, understanding.

"Lizzie, I got a girl pregnant last year," he murmured. My head shot up and he looked at me with a sad, regretful face.

"She didn't want the baby and hell, I don't make enough money to even live on my own, and so she found a place outside of Portsmouth, New Hampshire. Lizzie, I went with her and it was a good place. They were very nice to her, and although it was emotionally painful, they took really good care of her. They made sure she understood all her options, and when we went to the appointment, it was a really most comfortable place despite the reason we were there," he said.

"What happened to her?"

He shrugged his shoulders. "We're still friends. We'll always remember what happened, but she seems to be doing okay. She's dating a good guy and I'm happy for her. We were only together a few times and she was on the pill but no one ever told her that the antibiotics for her bronchitis would lower the strength of the birth control.

"Anyway, I'm telling you this because that place should be where you go. You'll feel as comfortable as you can. I still know where it is so we can look it up for you to call. You don't want to wait. They told her that the further you are along, the more painful it is," he said with certainty.

"I would really like that, Sean. Can we call today? I want to get it over with as soon as possible. Then I need to find a place to live since I don't think my family will ever want to see me again," I said with a cringe.

He squeezed my hand. Oh, how I loved Sean. He was always there for me, and at that moment, he was the only person I could fully trust. Knowing that he was there for me and with no ultimatum for himself, made him everything to me.

A half hour later, Sean got off the phone and handed me a slip of paper that he had scribbled on. It was the name of the clinic with the address and phone number. I looked down at the paper for a long while before I outstretched my hand to his phone. He sat down next to me on the bed and placed his hand on my knee, squeezing repeatedly.

I dialed the number and a kind voice answered. I took a deep breath.

"My name is Lizzie and I need to schedule an appointment for an…a…termination of pregnancy," I said, starting to feel stronger as I spoke.

"Yes, dear. How far along are you?" she asked with complete normalcy. Well, she was an assistant at an abortion clinic. Jesus, how can anyone work there? If I had to look at multiple people like me every day, I think I would cry every time I went home.

"I don't know. I also don't know the last time I got my period," I said.

"Okay, well, then it's important to see you as soon as possible because there's a period of time that is acceptable for this type of procedure," she said.

"Okay. I'm available whenever you have an appointment."

"Let me check the schedule and see when we can get you in next." She put me on hold and I listened to the soft jazz music over the phone. I hardly registered that Sean was still there, squeezing my knee. I looked at him and a tear fell down my hot cheeks. Never in a million years would I think I'd be there with Sean, making an appointment to get rid of another man's baby. My life was so surreal.

The woman came on the phone. "Lizzie?" she asked.

"Yes, I'm still here," I answered.

"Okay, we have a cancellation for next Thursday at one thirty. Can you come in then?" she asked.

"Yes," I said softly. "What do I need to do to prepare?"

"Good, you will be here about an hour. Please come in sweatpants or something comfortable for after the procedure. You'll be sore. We do a small therapy session to make sure you're not being forced into anything and you'll sign that you want to make this decision over any other. After that, you'll get a thorough exam to make sure you're still in your first trimester then the procedure will take about fifteen minutes," she said.

"So I pay and fill out the forms then? Do you need anything from me now?" I asked.

"You pay when you come here, and yes, you'll need to fill out other forms, all confidential, of course. All I need from you now is your full name and a phone number to reach you in case we need to move your appointment to another time." I rattled off my name and gave her Sean's number. Even if I wasn't there, he would get me any message I needed.

When I hung up the phone, I lay back on the bed again and listened to Pink Floyd's The Wall, pouring through all the speakers around the room. *Mother, do you think they dropped the bomb?* Sean lay back with me and we sang the song together softly. We didn't speak very much after that. He brought pillows down and plumped them under my head and we cuddled to the rest of the album. Eventually, after the exhausting day, both mentally and emotionally, I fell into a sound sleep that lasted through the next morning.

Sean's place became my refuge. The next morning, I got onto Sean's computer and logged into my Yahoo mail account. That there were five messages from Teagan. Email had never been my favorite way to talk to Teagan but the occasional email from him at work would show up in my inbox just to confirm our night's plans. I had forgotten to call him to let him know I wouldn't be going back. So much had transpired throughout the day, and the comfort of Sean's bedroom made me feel safe and secure. I was still lonely without Teagan's touch but the arctic wall between us was starting to harden now more than ever. It was Tuesday and his friend was coming into town the next day. I didn't see any reason to head back to Boston for one night with him.

I read over his emails.

Lizzie,

I tried ringing you at home and your brother said you aren't living there anymore. He was an asshole to me and I think he called me every swear word in the book. He wouldn't tell me where you went to, and even though I begged, he didn't give me any information. Please email me and tell me where you are and if you're okay. I need to hear from you.

201

T

The rest of the emails were similar but they came more frequently as the hours passed.

I hit reply to his last email.

Teagan,

I'm fine. My family isn't happy with me and the situation. They don't like the decision I've made so I suggest you don't call my house again. You're not one of their favorite people these days. I'm staying with a friend outside of Boston. I made an appointment for next Thursday at one thirty. The address is 4558 Main Street. Portsmouth, New Hampshire. I'm not sure when I'll be back in town but I do hope you have a great time with your friend. You don't need to worry about me. I'm safe. If you are coming with me next Thursday, let me know via email and I'll come pick you up. If you don't want to go, I have a friend that will.

Lizzie

I started surfing the internet. I wanted to see if there was any information on the clinic. I hoped it wasn't part of some strip mall or on a busy street. Sean came in with a steaming cup of coffee and I looked at him and smiled.

"Just the way you like it," Sean said as he settled on the bed with a hard rock magazine.

"You're so wonderful. Thank you, honey," I replied.

"So, how long will I be graced with your presence?" he asked, not looking up at me from the magazine.

"Honestly, I don't know. I would much rather get punched in the stomach than go through this," I said as I pointed up to the home screen of the clinic.

"Jesus Christ, Lizzie. Don't say shit like that," he said, giving me a stern look. "You can stay here as long as you want but I do have to work tonight. I have a few ink appointments."

As I clicked off the home page of the clinic, I didn't know what was going to happen to me there. I started to close out the Yahoo window when I saw a new message from Teagan.

Lizzie,

I'm not happy you didn't come back to me last night. I wanted to be there when you found out about the appointment. How far outside the city are you? I can come to you tonight. I won't see you until after Sunday and I miss you already. I'm so sorry this is happening to you, to us, baby. You're always on my mind. Please call me and find a way to see me tonight.

T

I hit reply.

Teagan,

I miss you, too. I'm doing okay but I'm too far outside the city, and it would be a long drive back and forth. I'll call you Monday and we can talk then.

Lizzie

Sean was looking over my shoulder, and as I closed out the window, I turned to see that his mouth was open.

"That's him?" he asked incredulously.

"Yes," I said.

"He says he fucking misses you? He got you knocked up then dismissed you and the—" I cut him off.

"Stop. I came to you because I knew you wouldn't have an opinion. I just need you as a friend and as much as he's hurt me, I went into this with my eyes open. Well, maybe half open. Neither one of us ever thought this would happen, but I know he still has feelings for me. He does," I reassured myself.

Sean coughed out, "bullshit."

I scowled at him. He gave me a sad smile.

"He only wanted to get in your pants, Lizzie. And who wouldn't? You're an amazing girl and you're beautiful and smart. You always have been," Sean said.

I looked at him, not knowing which to object to. Did Teagan only want in my pants the entire summer and even now that I'm pregnant? Am I an amazing, beautiful woman? I stuttered out a few groans and he smiled at me.

"Can we watch a movie?" I asked. "I need my mind off this shit right now," I said as I got up from his desk.

"*Fight Club* or *The Matrix*?" he asked.

"Number one rule of Fight Club!" I exclaimed.

He laughed and intertwined our fingers together before he knelt down in front of the DVD player to pop in the movie.

"I love you, you know," I said.

"Back atcha, babe," he said.

The time at Sean's seemed to straighten out my thinking. There were no influences. It was just me and my thoughts, which cleared every day. Sean went to work every night and I missed having someone to talk to, but when he came home, he always brought me ice cream and we watched a movie until the early hours in the morning. It was comforting, but Sean was not Teagan. I started to think more and more about how Teagan ruined me for every other man. I wanted to be grateful for every moment I spent with Teagan but I really wanted more. I wanted just one more month. Time was running out. Baby or not, I wanted to wake up to his hands stretched all over my body. I thought back to the last night we spent together and smiled. I pocketed that memory in the back of my mind for the future. As pathetic as it sounded, I wanted whatever he would give me for the rest of his time in Boston and when I went to visit him in Ireland. The future was not dim. I could make my future any way I wanted, and if I couldn't live without him, I'd follow him. I'd beg. Oh God. I was so messed up.

Twenty-Seven

The Greatest Blow

Still at Sean's on Wednesday morning, my heart squeezed in longing. There was no way I could go to Teagan until Sunday, which I realized happened to be only two weeks before he actually flew back to Ireland. His friend from university was coming into town and he wanted to spend every night with him, not to mention he didn't have the room for two guests. Some of the other guys were also having friends come so I understood from our previous conversations that I wasn't welcomed. I would be okay. I had a lot on my plate anyway. I couldn't help but think that he was pulling away from me. After all the turmoil he had witnessed me go through, I'm sure he wanted to spend his last days in Boston without the constant reminder of me and the pregnancy. I didn't ask him to go with me to my appointment at the clinic. I just gave him the option. It was up to him whether or not he wanted to be there for me. He said several times that he wouldn't let me go alone and he wanted to drive me home after. I was happy he would be there. He seemed like the only appropriate choice, after all.

After being at Sean's for days, I felt like I was overstaying my welcome although Sean would've never let me leave if he knew I felt that way. Nonetheless, I decided to call my oldest friend, Shannon, first thing the next morning to let her know that I was going through a hard break up and my parents were being assholes. I told her that I was staying at Sean's. She quickly came up with an excuse to go to Boston from New York City, where she worked as an assistant to an assistant to an assistant to some fashion mogul. She told me what train she would take that day.

"Let's go to Mamma Mia!" she exclaimed. I let go of the breath I had been holding. She didn't broach the subject of the break up or my parents. I could tell she just wanted me to have some fun to get it out of my mind.

"Don't they have that on or off Broadway?" I asked, smiling. I was trying to be at least a little normal on the outside. Fake it until you make it and all that shit.

Shannon was a dear friend. She saw me go through so much in high school, and yet we always got stuck together. Like Sean, I would often flee to her house for extended stays and her single mom was always happy to have me. I missed her like crazy. I never wanted to live in New York City, but if there was one reason I would move there, it would be only for her.

"Yes, but we need to see it together. We know all the words and we can pretend we're in Muriel's Wedding. It will be a blast. We can stay at Mom's and have a sleepover. Weeee. It will be so much fun!"

I told Sean she was coming down, and because he was feeling a little overprotective of me, he insisted on going to Boston with me. When I told him we were going to a show and he immediately refused, telling me to have a great time. It wasn't until after lunch with Sean in Newburyport that I said goodbye to him. He asked if I would return and I told him I was homeless so I probably would. I drove down to the train station to pick her up and we immediately went to Faneuil Hall to get the day tickets to the show. We went to the bathroom and prettied up for the night's events.

Hours later, we came out of the theater, still singing.

"Where should we go?" she asked.

"Uppity or regular pub?" I asked.

"Duh. Uppity. The Greatest Bar," she announced.

"I just rolled my eyes," I said, laughing.

When we walked into the loud and crowded bar, we noticed two stools at the counter and immediately took them. Shannon ordered a martini and I ordered a diet coke. I swiveled around and scanned the bar to see if there were any familiar faces.

"Hold my seat. I have to go to the bathroom," I said, sliding off my stool.

As I headed towards the ramp up to the restrooms, I stopped still. I felt sucker punched. I couldn't breathe. I couldn't move. I… I…

There, half way up the red carpeted ramp, I saw the back of Teagan's beautiful head. He wasn't paying any attention to his surroundings. Everyone around him was casually talking but his head nuzzled into the dark, curly hair of a petite girl. He kissed her bare shoulder as she looked up to him with adoring eyes. I was sick.

I tried so hard to look away but like the aftermath of a car accident, I couldn't stop. I even craned my neck beyond people walking around me. Just then, I saw Freddie. He stood stunned then immediately jumped over the rail of the ramp. The several steps from the ramp to me were lightning fast.

Freddie stood right in front of me, fully blocking me from the view of Teagan. I stood there shaking, eyes wide open and my hand covering my mouth to prevent myself from throwing up. The pit of my stomach rose up to my chest then up to my eyes.

Tears flooded my vision as Freddie put his hands on my shoulder and looked straight into my eyes.

"It's not what you think, Lizzie," Freddie said sternly.

I stammered while trying to catch the air from my chest. I looked at him and turned, confused.

"Huh?" I asked.

"Lizzie, that's his girlfriend, Moira. They are together at university," he replied. He said it like I already knew about her. He was trying to explain that it wasn't some random girl but his girlfriend that I must have known about all along.

"Girlfriend," I stated, stunned. After my initial shock, I gave him the biggest "What the Fuck?" look. Freddie knew he had a fucking girlfriend? Did they all know? After all this time, I never knew. I never fucking knew.

"Oh my God, Lizzie. You, you didn't know? Moira and Teagan have been on and off for years. They grew up together," he replied sadly.

"I think they're back on again." I laughed with no amusement.

As Freddie slowly nodded his head, I glanced over his shoulder and my eyes met Cian's. He glanced at me and Freddie for an instant and hastily made his way over to Teagan. Cian barely even whispered something in Teagan's ear before Teagan whirled around and pointedly looked at me. His chin dropped and his face turned blank, almost impassive. I screamed inside and I couldn't think about what to do. I looked back at Freddie and put my hands on his arms as if he was grounding me. The bar was swallowing me whole and Freddie was my only anchor. Then I regained my inner courage, I pushed Freddie rather hard and yelled, "You son of a bitch. You lied to me, Freddie! You fucking lied to me. I thought we were friends. I can understand HIS intentions," I said, pointing towards Teagan. "But what are yours? Why would you never say a fucking thing to me?"

Freddie glanced back towards the ramp and looked at me guiltily.

"Lizzie, please don't make a scene. She doesn't know about you either. He just told us tonight to keep you a secret. What the hell did you think he was doing when he asked you to stop coming around? Do you know how many times I picked up the phone to try to see you? I wanted to talk to you. I feel responsible. But this wasn't my secret to tell. You were with him and I just assumed you knew he was kind of involved," he said.

I scoffed at him and took a step back like he slapped me. None of me being with Teagan was my idea. He propositioned me. He made me feel special. He tried so hard in the beginning. He was the father of my… My tears were finally dried up, so I wiped under my eyes very quickly and turned to leave. As I walked out the door, I grabbed my purse off the stool and told Shannon I was leaving. I don't even know if she heard me. She was laughing and I never looked back as I walked out the door to a hot and humid night. Freddie ran out the door right after me.

As I started vigorously walking down the street to my car, Freddie groaned. Where did I go wrong with Freddie? He could have been my constant through this whole summer had Teagan let me be his friend. It was all bitterness just then. He wouldn't ever understand what just happened to me. I could hear him telling me we need to sit down to talk in the background of my thoughts. I couldn't hear him. He needed to leave me alone. I lost all of my friends. All of them. They were all gone. The summer was all gone. Did he think he could say anything that would make it all better? I prayed in that moment he would just know. I prayed that he would know that I was hurting more about this than any other moment in time. Teagan would never take the blame, he would never admit to anything. Freddie could never know and for fuck's sake, everyone needed to know that I was pregnant with Teagan's baby. I prayed Freddie could read my thoughts. I lost it all. I lost. Game over.

"Lizzie, wait! Please talk to me. Tell me you're going to be okay," he said.

I whirled around to him and my pain was so evident that I couldn't even look at him.

"Do I look okay, Freddie? That mother fucker screwed me all summer long, both physically and mentally. He did it on purpose. That selfish piece of shit has no soul, no heart, and no conscious. Or maybe that is all Irishmen, hmmm?" I asked with one eyebrow cocked.

My whole body was trembling. Why couldn't I just shut down and not feel anything? I was so good at that before I met Teagan. I could climb into bed and feel nothing. I would normally brush this whole thing off and chalk it up to another misstep in my life. But he got me pregnant. I had to endure that awful first few days in his arms. I was losing my whole family. I had nowhere to go. I looked around at the people walking by and wished I was anywhere else, anyone else. What about Teagan? He hadn't lost anything. He stole everything and went on living like I was nothing.

Freddie blanched at me and turned himself out to the street and stood silent. Under his breath, he muttered, "You should have picked me that night."

"What?" I screamed at him. He was going to be straight with me.

"You should have fucking picked me. I wanted you this whole summer and you chose that bastard. I tried so many times to tell you. Remember my birthday? Jesus, Lizzie, I fell in love with you that night, playing the guitar and on the train. I think about you all the time, and now I have to fucking watch you crumble because of him." He cried out, pain in his throat.

"Why don't you tell her what you really think, Freddie?" Teagan said with steadfast calm out from behind us.

I whirled around and stared at him in disbelief.

"Who the fucking shit is she, Teagan?" I yelled.

Freddie came up behind me and placed his arm on mine and murmured for me to calm down. Teagan walked towards me and stood a foot away from my face and said, "She's an old friend."

"A friend? A fucking friend? Do you kiss all your friends on their necks while groping their backsides?" I asked incredulously.

He grimaced.

"Oh wait, yes. Yes, you do. Because we are friends, right, Teagan? Summer friends. You are leaving so we could never be anything more but you never once even hinted that you had a girlfriend back home. Don't fucking lie to me. Freddie already told me about her so your explanation means shit to me." I held up my hand like that was all I needed to say.

Instead, I went on. I pointed at his face and seethed, "Do you think I would have even let you touch me if I knew you had a girlfriend? Do you think I would have even entertained the idea that you were someone I wanted to get to know as a friend? The minute I knew Cian had a girlfriend, I never looked at him the same. Off limits. This American girl, or so you call me, is not that kind of girl, and fuck you for using me and disrespecting everything that happened between us." I motioned to my belly where he implanted a baby in me. Bonded.

He didn't miss my point.

He gave me a pained look and whispered, "She hasn't been my girlfriend all summer. I came here and she went to Paris. I don't know what she did there and she certainly doesn't know about my relationship here. I'm sorry, Lizzie. I never wanted to hurt you."

"Hurt me? Hurt me? You think me knowing now that you have a girlfriend hurts me? No, it fucking breaks me into crackled specks of dust. It makes every moment I shared with you and I mean, every God damn moment I shared with you, a lie. You are the most manipulative, self serving bastard I've ever met and believe me, I have met myself many times," I said with rage.

"I never wanted you to know, Lizzie. I'm sorry. You, we were just for the summer. She and I have been forever," he said.

Freddie cursed under his breath, and when I turned to look at him, he was bent over with his hands on his knees like he was going to vomit.

I threw up my arms. "Well, then, get going. Go back to her and start your fucking forever now. I'm not going to spoil anything for you because I have enough sympathy for that poor girl. She will never know the true beast that lives inside you." My whole body was trembling harder and I wanted to go stand with Freddie and puke, too.

He hung his head and muttered, "Lizzie."

I popped my eyes open, and in a voice I'd never heard come from myself before, said, "You aren't allowed to address me by my fucking name ever again." I clipped each word out so he knew that I no longer existed in his life, nor he in mine.

Freddie came up and put a soft arm around my waist to steady my shaking body and Teagan looked at Freddie, dumbfounded.

"Teagan, it's time for you to go back inside. You've done enough to her. Let it go, man," Freddie said with a scowl.

The tears started again and I couldn't understand why. I was so furious, but Freddie's gentle hand on me made me feel the pain of Teagan's lost touch. Never again would he kiss my lips or entwine our fingers together. Never again would he whisper that he wanted me and I was the most special girl in his life. He would never look at me the way Freddie was looking at me.

Teagan started to say something back to Freddie. It was obvious Teagan wanted to get into a shit storm fight with the look on his face. He wasn't going to back down and that was so confusing. How could he even think about fighting for me when there was another woman waiting for him in the bar? I cut him off by holding up my hand.

"Don't you ever fucking look or even touch me again. You don't have anything to say to anyone about me. You just lost the right to even think about me. You obviously don't care about me. I gave you my complete trust and you just stomped all over it. Freddie has and always will be a trustworthy friend. But you? " I questioned and shook my head. "Leave."

Out of the corner of my eye, I saw his pretty girlfriend in her innocent little dress and black curls, standing right outside the door, looking perplexed. She had obviously heard my last sentence, and slowly, her hand went to her mouth.

I leaned into Teagan's ear and took one last whiff of him and whispered, "Look there, Teag. Karma is a fucking bitch."

Teagan flew around to find her standing there. Immediately, he rushed over to her and drew her close, shuffling her through the door, never looking back at me.

I turned into Freddie's arms, and he rubbed my back lightly up and down for what seemed like an hour. But even in his comforting arms, he was not Teagan. The pain of his loss seeped in and the bereft took on its force. I pulled away from Freddie and gave him a slight smile.

"I have to go now," I said quietly.

"Okay, Lizzie. Can I call you?"

"I don't think it's a good idea right now, Freddie. Plus, I need to figure out what all this was, what it means now," I said.

He looked at me with sad eyes.

I put my arm on his shoulder and kissed him on his mouth tenderly.

"Good bye, Freddie," I whispered. He tried to pull on my arm but I forcefully pulled it from his grasp and started away from him and from all the hurt of the night.

I walked to my car three blocks down from the bar, and started to bawl. I don't remember when Shannon got to the car, but she immediately pulled me out of the driver's seat and peeled the car out onto the road home.

"Shannon, one stop before we head to your house," I said.

She looked over to me with concern. I gave her Teagan's address. When we got to his apartment, I got out of the car before she turned off the ignition. I ran up the stairs and used my keys to let myself in. Shannon caught the door before it could close and continued to ask what we were doing.

I immediately ran down the dark hallway to Teagan's room and flipped the lights on. Woman's clothes were all over Teagan's bed, and I clutched my gut. I went into the closet, our fucking sleep pad, and went to the place where we kept the condoms. I pulled out all of them and threw half of them at Shannon. She gave me a quizzical look.

"Rip them all open," I said. "He never fucking slept with her. It isn't in his traditions," I said as I air quoted the word traditions.

She smiled and started to rip. Every condom came out and we stretched them open and threw them all over the bed. Shannon disappeared for a minute, and when she came back, she said, "I've always wanted to do that."

A carton of eggs were in her hands, and I smiled at her as I pulled out the last condom and tucked it into the bra at the end of the bed. She handed me three eggs and we quickly put them under the sheets and pillows. I threw a few in Teagan's shoes in the closet and Shannon ran out to put the carton in the trash, making it seem that nothing was out of the ordinary. They would find out when they returned to this room. That made me smile wickedly. Fucking revenge.

As we walked out, I threw the keys to the apartment on the kitchen bar before we left with the door wide open. I didn't care if they were robbed. I already knew what it felt like to be exposed and torn apart, and I was certainly going to get over it. That Thursday afternoon at the clinic would be the perfect time to rid him from my soul.

Twenty-Eight

Goodbye Nobody

Sunday afternoon, I took Shannon back to the train so she could go home to New York before her hectic work week. I could tell that she was resistant to leave me after what she witnessed outside the bar on Friday. I didn't want to share anymore details with her after that, so she kept me entertained with movies and music. She squeezed me tight and made me promise to call her anytime I needed an ear to listen. I also had a hectic week ahead of me, and while I was sure it would be different from hers, I knew it would be a far more memorable one.

Shannon made sure I called Sean to let him know I would be returning to his apartment that afternoon. I could tell from his voice that he was worried and grateful I was coming back to him. I didn't tell him what I learned on Friday for fear he would defend me in some way. I would try my best to calmly tell him and let him know I would remain strong without Teagan's support during the coming days.

When I pulled up to his apartment, he was already sitting on the steps with a coffee cup and his rocker magazine. He looked up and quickly came to my side, grabbing the big bag from my passenger seat and wrapping his other arm around me.

"It felt lonely without you here this weekend," he said. "I've been thinking a lot about you not having a place to stay, so I talked with my roommate and you can live here as long as you need to."

I hugged him fiercely and rubbed his warm back. "Thank you, Sean. It's hard to believe I don't have anywhere to go anymore."

He sighed and reminded me that he was there and I was certainly not homeless. His grip around my waist was gentle and the comfort of knowing that someone cared for me, even through this tragic time, felt nice. It wasn't everything I'd ever hoped for, but knowing that I had a couple good friends no matter what was just enough for me to start crying.

"I can't live with you, Sean. I need to spend a few days with you but I have school and I need to stop living for other people. I'm a puppet to everyone in my life. I go where I'm wanted and I don't even fucking want myself right now. I need to find a place in my heart to become strong again, if I ever have been," I said through my tears.

He nodded and brought me inside, quickly making me a cup of coffee then putting my bag in his room.

"Are you nervous?" he asked tentatively.

"Yes. But not for the reasons you may think. I'm nervous about what will happen after I heal from the procedure, if I ever do. I'm not making this choice lightly. It's my baby I'm killing and I don't think I'll ever get over that, no matter if I ever have children again. This baby should have been a blessing, not a curse. A curse that has torn my whole circle of people apart," I said solemnly.

I went to lay on his bed, fatigued and emotional. He sat at the end of it, going through his CD cases. I watched his back and started to talk.

"You can't turn around and look at me as I tell you about something that happened on Friday when I was with Shannon," I said.

He quickly turned his head to look at me and I gave him the "Don't fuck with me" look. He turned back slowly and popped in a Counting Crows CD. I immediately told him to turn that fucking music off. He jumped at my anger and replaced it with Led Zeppelin.

"Talk," he said, never looking back at me.

"Shannon and I went to a bar in Boston after the show. I found Teagan and his roommates there. Teagan wasn't alone. His friend, evidently, is his girlfriend from Ireland. She was cute. She was nothing like me. I could tell that he adored her, and his body language told me she was the most important person in his life. I blew up. I said things to him that I'll never fucking regret. I could see his anguish but I didn't care. He was nobody to me anymore and yet, he's still everything. I don't know if I'll ever get over him, even if he's in love with someone else. I suppose this is what Chase feels like right now. The irony of it all is that I told Teagan that karma is a bitch and yet, maybe karma came back to bite me in the ass, after all," I said with a realization.

He sat there for several moments, waiting for me to say more, but I didn't. I sat up and put my arms around him and whispered, "I'm so scared of living my life now." He tugged on my hands and kissed the palms of both.

"I understand that feeling, Lizzie. We all go through shit that we regret but this wasn't your fault. You fell in love with a man that couldn't ever love you back," he said. "I felt the same way for a girl once and I didn't know how to tell her. I just didn't want to ever be away from her. When she moved to Oregon, I didn't know how to live my life. But I figured it out. I let go and the pain slowly dwindled."

I looked at him over his shoulder and smiled. "You know that we would have killed each other by now, Sean. You're so important to me that after everything I've been through, I would never want that for us," I said.

He laughed then choked.

"What a fucking asshole you got yourself mixed up with," he said.

"I know," I whispered. "No accent will ever tempt this girl again."

"Can I go with you to the appointment? Please," he begged.

I shook my head and gave him a warm smile. "I can't depend on anyone but myself now."

He nodded. The discussion was over. But inside my head, I continued on. It was time to fucking grow up. Gone was my youth. Gone were my carefree times. Gone was the man who tore my body and soul apart. All I had left was absolutely and completely nothing. I had no pride. One word couldn't possible encompass what I felt but if I had to choose just one, it would be ashamed. But one quote kept coming back in my mind. No matter where you go, there you are.

We spent the next three days as we had the previous week. Listening to music started to heal my soul. Listening to Sean's even breathing while he slept gave me solace. Listening to comedy movies and forcing a laugh reminded me that life goes on. Life would never feel complete without Teagan in it, but it didn't matter anymore. I would eventually turn that situation into much more, and I would pay retribution to the world in some way.

Early Thursday afternoon came too quickly and my head was swimming with doubt and insecurity. My body trembled everywhere, but my heart screamed the most. After packing my bags and a quick kiss to Sean, promising I would call him that night, I left towards the clinic.

As I drove, I thought about nothing. All I did was feel the absolute torture of fear. The clinic was an old house turned into a medical facility. I parked my car under the big oak trees in the small parking lot and took a deep breath. When I made it to the steps, I was immediately frozen with fear. Two armed guards looked at me with a small smile. One man stepped forward and asked me for my driver's license while the other one held a clipboard of papers.

"Elizabeth O'Malley," the guard said, holding my ID.

The other guard nodded and made some sort of note on the sheet. As the guard handed me back my ID, he quickly scanned the area. I could tell they had problems in the past and I was relieved that these men cared enough for my choice to stand guard. At least someone was.

The first officer punched in a code to the door and opened it for me. He went inside and gave the woman at reception my name. I was solely focused on the woman as she looked down at her papers and nodded.

"You have a few papers to fill out, honey. I have a clipboard here, and since your procedure has already been paid for, we won't need anything more than that," she said.

"What? Paid for?" I asked in astonishment.

"Yes. The young man accompanying you is already in the seating area to the left."

"I don't have anyone accompanying me today," I said.

"Oh. Well, then, there must be a miscommunication. Here, let me meet you around in the sitting room and we'll get your forms and payment in order," she said.

I walked tentatively towards the room and scanned it slowly, looking for Sean or Conner, but in the far corner, Teagan sat with his elbows on his knees, looking intently at me. I stared back at him with utter shock. He looked so tired. He looked so amazing. He looked like mine. He stood up to take a step towards me and I stepped back. The receptionist came around the corner and pointed her finger towards Teagan.

"That young man is who paid today. Is he… do you know him?" she asked.

"Yes." I scowled.

She didn't miss my tone of voice. "Do you want him to be removed?" she asked.

I thought for a long moment. First, what the mother fucking hell was he doing there? Second, how did he get there? Third, do I want him removed? The question held more meaning than she would ever know.

I shook my head slowly, took the clipboard and went to sit silently next to Teagan. There was that arctic wall again and he made no move to comfort me. He stayed silent while watching me sit then start to finger the forms. I made sure my arm didn't brush over his. I made sure not to make eye contact. I slowly filled out the forms, and when I was done, I put them on my lap and reclined back into my seat, taking in the surroundings. Only one other girl was in the room and she didn't look like she was there for a termination. Perhaps she was waiting on someone?

Just then, I registered that music was playing through the office. It was David Gray. "This Year's Love." Teagan and I both looked at each other in shock. We grabbed each other's hands and just stared at one another while we listen and held on to every word. *This year's love had better last. Heaven knows it's high time. I've been waiting on my own too long.*

I shook my head out of the daze. Out of the irony. Out of my mind. A nurse came in and asked me to follow her back. I stood, releasing his hand for the last time, and moved forward after her.

Everything went in slow motion as the hustle of the nurses and doctor scurried around the sterile room. After meeting with the therapist for a very short time and ensuring that this was what I wanted, she nodded and led me back to the operation room. I took in the sterile surroundings. The stainless steel trays of instruments, the stirrups of the table that I would lay on, the tubes and machines neatly gathered around the area that I assumed would be where the doctor sat. The therapist told me to remove everything from the waist down and cover the rest of my body with a plastic cloth.

Now the nurses were pulling things out of plastic, sterile envelopes and needles were drawn out and placed on the steel tray. I started to shake and opened my mouth to ask questions but soon there were two nurses by the head of the table, lightly rubbing my arms. Up and down. Up and down.

One nurse was very quiet as she told me what to expect.

"The doctor is going to check your uterus to make sure you aren't too late in getting this procedure done. He'll insert the clamps, like a regular visit, and it may be a little cold but you will get used to it very soon," she said.

I felt the clamps and gasped. It'd been a really long time since I had gone to an OBGYN so it felt so foreign to me. He murmured something about being ten weeks along. I thought to myself. Ten weeks? No, that can't be right. The condom broke well after that. Holy shit, it wasn't because of the condom. I sat up and the nurses held me down like I was a prisoner.

"I have to tell Teagan it wasn't because we broke the condom," I said frantically.

"Soon," the other nurse said.

"Now the doctor is going to inject you with a medicine that will numb you so you won't feel as much discomfort," the nurse said in gentle tones.

I could feel the needle. It was so painful, tears welled in my eyes. I closed them to blank out what was happening. I tried to think of anyplace but there and imagined myself safely tucked underneath my sheets in my bed at home. It would be so warm. This place was so cold. It felt like I was crackling under its intense frozen environment.

Then I felt cramping. I looked up to see the nurse looking at the doctor, who nodded.

"He has just opened your cervix to allow access to your uterus. It will be painful but we're right here if you need to squeeze our hands," she said.

Oh my God, oh my God. The pain was indescribable. It felt like they were ripping my insides out. Exposed. Never in my life had I felt such agony and I cried out with every inch of me. I felt semi-conscious and the wrecked feeling was worse than any death I could ever imagine for myself.

When I heard the sucking machine turn on, I froze and sat up straight. No, no, no. No sucking. No vacuum.

"Stop!" I yelled.

The doctor sat back and smiled gently at me. "It won't be for a few more minutes, Lizzie. Then you'll be safe and warm." I was sobbing by then, clamping my legs together and fiercely shaking my head. "No! Stop! I need a few minutes."

I heard the vacuum machine turn off and the nurses murmuring to me about taking a few minutes to gather myself as the doctor sat back and read over a chart. My heart raced, the cramping never dulling, and then I felt the worse pain and guilt I'd ever felt in my entire life.

Fifteen minutes later, I ran out of the room, still pulling up my sweatpants. I went straight out the door to the warm air. It was so warm and inviting. It was all over but as much as I made the decision to follow through, I was still so confused and no one could penetrate me.

Strong arms came around my sides and Teagan kissed my head. I struggled out of his embrace and started to my car.

"Lizzie! Wait a minute!"

I whirled on him. "What are you doing here, Teagan?"

He gave me an incredulous look. "I'm here for you. I didn't want you to be alone," he said.

"Well, get used to the idea because I am alone. I've been alone forever. Now you can leave," I said sternly.

He flinched. "I thought I could drive you home. Do you feel okay? Are you…"

"I. Am. Fine," I said, "and no, you won't take me home. You won't take me anywhere. I have a hotel nearby and I'll stay the night there," I lied. "Now, get the fuck out of my life. You only hurt me. Don't you see that? I wanted, wanted more from you, and you squashed me. You fucking tore me apart and so did they," I said as I pointed back at the clinic.

His eyes followed my arm then back to me. His look was of regret, sorrow, and guilt.

"Lizzie, I never wanted to hurt you," he said pleadingly.

"No," I said with resolve, "let me finish."

He stood there, looking just as beautiful as the last time I saw him...without her. His blue eyes pierced my heart and I caught my breath. It was so hard to fucking breathe. Pain was the monster of my soul, and I was determined to find the way that led me away from it.

"You've been letting go from me for a long time. Perhaps, you let go of the idea of me all together when we took our first hike together. You had the advantage this entire summer and I've never let anyone have an advantage over me. So, now you have to allow me to let go. You need to cut the last cord. Just cut me out. You don't have to think about the baby anymore. You don't have to think about the losses we both suffered. I will always do the thinking for the both of us. Knowing that you'll be happy when you move back to your girlfriend will be the only reason I will ever be able to get over this summer. I'll never forget what this summer did to me. So, stop trying to make this right. It was never right. The only way you can help me is to let go. To walk away. Stop thinking about me. Stop following me. Just stop. Maybe one day I'll remember the good times we had together. For now, I am wrecked. I have to find my way back to peace. The thought of even loving someone like I've loved you pains me because I don't know if it'll ever be possible and that's not the life I want. Can you understand that? Can you find it in you to believe that I don't need you? I never did. I wanted you. It's just that you never wanted me. Unrequited love is what tears peoples' souls apart." I stopped and knew tears were streaming down my face, down my neck, down my shirt. I didn't care. I was bare. Raw. Nothing he could say or do at that point would make me believe in anything good in the world. Nothing he said or did would make me believe in me again. It was over.

I turned around and walked towards my car. As I opened the door, I saw him standing there, tears in his eyes, and I put my hand up in a silent goodbye. I got into my car and drove home to Wellesley, ready to face my family and push myself back into the only place I belonged.

Twenty-Nine

After the Loss

I ran up the stairs to my front door, and for the first time in my life, I knocked. My mother immediately opened the door and stood there, shocked to see me. She raced forward and embraced me so tightly, I couldn't breathe. My mother looked so much older than I'd ever seen her. Her gray hairs came out in the sunshine and I took in her familiar scent. She was love and I needed it. I needed her.

"Oh, my baby. We've been so worried about you," she cried as she put her hand over her mouth. "God, we made you go. You left. You never called and we've been so worried. We haven't slept. I wanted to be there for you, Lizzie. I wanted to talk to you. I overreacted and I am so sorry. You are so important to me. Please don't leave again. Please let me help." She was sobbing and I couldn't bear her pain. No one else should feel an ounce of the pain I felt.

I trembled in her arms, and with tears rolling down my face, I held her. I held on so tight that I felt her inside and out. The pain I had caused them all of these years was excruciating. I never thought of others. Never. Thank fuck they still loved me, even knowing I needed to have an abortion.

"Mom, I couldn't do it. The baby. The pregnancy. I…" She cut me off.

"We love you no matter what you do. I'll call your father and brother down. They've been so anxious. I've been reading up on what to do after an abortion and I can be here for you," she said in a rush.

I shook my head.

"It's okay, Mom. Can we please talk later? I am so tired and I just need to lie down."

Conner came down and gave me a relieved smile. He tucked me under his chin and whispered how much he loved me and nothing would ever come between us again. I laughed and told him to stop fooling himself. He laughed along with me but I could tell it was a choked laugh. He was crying too and Conner never cried. I held him tight and whispered how much I loved him. I couldn't believe I had put him in so many situations that could destroy his reputation. He was wonderful. He was the best brother that anyone could imagine and I nearly broke it all up in a million pieces.

Mom and Conner took me to my room, which was cleaner than I'd ever seen it. Mom had been busy. Books were stacked next to my bed and a brand new CD player sat next to them. They'd been taking care of me, even when I was gone. They tucked me in my bed and my mom sat and rubbed my feet as she whispered how glad she was that I came home. My father stood in the doorway, and when I looked up to him, he was crying. He didn't make a move towards me but I could feel the love spread across the room. He nodded and turned around with his head hung in emotion.

Days blurred together as the cramping finally subsided and I started to feel better. I was still sick inside but my family made sure I ate and got enough rest. They were amazing. I never felt more cared for.

Conner came in one day and pulled the ringing phone out of its socket with one pull. He cursed underneath his breath and took the phone out of my room, never looking at me. I knew the phone was ringing a lot but he startled me to my feet and I ran after him.

"Conner, what the fuck?" I asked.

"That mother fucking God damn son of a bitch piece of fucking shit keeps calling. He wants to know how you are, and every time I tell him to mind his own fucking business and stop harassing this family, he calls back an hour later," he roared.

I smiled at him and said, "So stop answering the fucking phone." I squeezed him tight with a smile, and he relaxed in my arms.

"God, Lizzie, I'm so glad you're home. You are so special and so fucking smart. You have your whole life ahead of you and nothing that has happened over the summer will change that. We have a plan and you'll feel good again soon. You just need a little help. We aren't going to push you but things have to change now."

I released him and nodded. "Conner, I know. Things are going to change dramatically. But, this summer… This summer was my bottom. It was the ultimate test of my self-worth and I failed," I said. "I'm finally going to settle into myself, and I'm trying to recognize that I'm not alone. I have my family and my friends and this time, I'm not going to do what I always do. I'm not going to run from myself."

He gave me a warm kiss on my cheek and walked away with the phone and broken cord in hand.

He turned back to me and said, "You know? I told him once over the phone that he better not hurt you or I would kick his little arse. I guess I wasn't very clear about that." He frowned and looked down at the floor. My eyes started to tear up and I hiccupped on a sob as I watched my brother try to decide how to fix me. Eventually, he figured out he couldn't. I was completely broken. I quietly closed my door and fell to the ground in tears. The downstairs phone started to ring again. I looked up to my guitar and began to write the sweetest lullaby for the baby Teagan never wanted.

"Teagan's Lullaby" was the only song I sung for months. I watched his plane take off from a distant parking lot in Boston. I knew I would never see him again. I cried myself to sleep that day, and when I woke up, I was numb. I couldn't move on for months. The memories of Teagan seeped into my bones and stayed there. All I could do was listen to David Gray and cry. I thought about those days we spent in bed. Those days we spent on the island. Those nights when he couldn't keep his hands off me haunted my dreams. I would sleep for days just so I could see his face, smiling at me. The few pictures that were taken of us together pained me so I hid them in the back of the closet. I was never the person he wanted. I wasn't the person he needed. It was a fake truth for him. For me, it was the truest love I'd ever known. Being alone never felt worse and all I wanted was him. I couldn't drink. I couldn't drive down Commonwealth Avenue. I couldn't breathe. I knew Teagan would always be with me and it would be impossible for me to ever forget him. Forget us. It was our summer fling that turned into so much more. I couldn't change the past. I couldn't change his past or his future. I was the present. He was my present. I told him to let me go but I knew it would be impossible. He wouldn't ever contact me again and he would move on. But I knew I never would.

EPILOGUE

2002

I took the ticket from the stewardess and put it back into my purse as I walked down the hall to the open plane. I started for the first class seats and closed in behind my son, still sleeping in his car seat. He had been restless all night. No matter his mood, I knew I would look back on this trip and be so proud of myself for making it.

I flipped my cell phone open and called Nick, my tall and gorgeous friend. I met Nick three months after Niall was born while on a lunch break from my awesome job in the financial district. He made me laugh when I wanted to sob.

"Hey, Lizzie. How's it going?" he asked with concern.

"Oh, well, you know, Niall is enjoying the free liquor and food in first class, and I am trying to get some rest. We're doing as well as expected on a long flight with a sixteen month old," I replied.

Nick laughed on the other end.

"How is Kathleen?" I asked. Kathleen was Nick's latest girlfriend and I found it safer to live vicariously through his love life. I could never fall in love again. It hurt too much. Guy friends were so much safer. Sean and Nick had been the rocks in my life these past two years.

"She's fine. We went to that sushi place last night. It was good." He sighed.

I laughed. He was so going to break up with her in the next few weeks. He just didn't know it yet.

233

"Hey! I'm going to miss you," he exclaimed.

"Me too. So, we're in D.C. The flight from Boston was easy. We should land in Cork by, umm, tomorrow, their time?" I asked, already confused by the time difference.

"You know, Liz, you don't have to do this," he said.

"I want to. I'm not going to make waves. I just want to see where he is from. Maybe…maybe it will bring me closure." I sighed.

I looked over at Niall and caressed his cheek with the back of my index finger.

"Well, call when you land. In the meantime, I'm counting the days until you're home," he said.

I laughed and told him to get laid. I turned off my phone when the steward asked me to.

Niall was born in 2001, the year the Twin Towers crumbled to the ground. He was a light in the darkness, in my darkness. The world around me suffered from one of the biggest tragedies in history, and while it pained me as well, my greatest secret still made me suffer daily. I remember the first time I held Niall in my arms. In that moment, I knew I was a better person. I would have a future with purpose and I felt settled. I would hold onto to my red headed, fair skinned son and make sure he never suffered any tragedies within my control. Being a mother changed everything. Teagan changed everything.

Flipping through the book, I found the world map of where every hub was. I traced the map lines of flights from Boston to Washington, D.C. and then I stopped. For two years, when I looked at a map, I always covered my hand over Ireland.

Perhaps it was to cherish the homeland of my family or maybe I just wanted to hide it like it never existed. I didn't feel that need any more though. I purposely traced the line from D.C. to Cork, Ireland, where I would try to find answers without causing any trouble. Teagan didn't need to know I was there. In fact, I was sure he didn't even live in Cork anymore. I'd never visited and I saw it fitting that Niall join me on the trip. My connection to Ireland seemed therapeutic after all I had been through.

Niall woke up and looked over to me. "Mama," he said, grabbing for me. I started to rub his belly. He loved that so much.

"Yes, honey. Mama loves you. Let me tell you a little secret. Did you know that you have Irish in your blood? I think you'll fit right in." I hummed to him with a smile.

"Yes, Niall, but you'll always be my American boy. That's the most important thing." I closed the magazine, put it away, and leaned back in my chair as the plane took off towards the home of the Irishmen I used to know.

Coming in May 2014

Lizzie O'Malley is back with a purpose in life. Still flighty and unpredictable, she knows that loving and losing Teagan Gallagher has changed her life forever. As she navigates her new life in Boston as a full time working mother, she promises herself she will never fall in love again.

But can she keep that promise after meeting Nick Sawyer, the gorgeous Texan who has fallen for her?

Follow Lizzie to Ireland where she struggles with tragedy and rediscovers herself all over again.

UNREQUITED

RELEASE IN AUGUST 2014

If you enjoy the books by Alisa Mullen, you can follow her!

Facebook Fan Page - http://tinyurl.com/l5jgo2b

Goodreads Page - http://tinyurl.com/m69qsof

Amazon BIO Page - http://tinyurl.com/l9plrxr

Twitter - @alimullenbooks